Upside Down
IN
Love

This book is a work of fiction. All names, characters, locations, and incidents are products of the author's imaginations. Any resemblance to actual person's, things, living or dead, locales, or events is entirely coincidental.

The strongest actions for a woman to take is to love herself. Be

herself and shine amongst those who never believed she could...

1

#golddigger

First, I blame you, then I want you

Fucking hate you, then I love you

I can't help myself, no

When I have you, wanna leave you

If you go, that's when I need you

I can't help myself no

"You come in waves," her soft voice murmured quietly while gazing straight ahead.

Chilled air blasted through the vents cooling off her mahogany hued skin as she lowered the volume on her radio. Her hooded eyes the same shade as honey peered openly at the large estate before her. This was the last place she wanted to be, but she had to get her sons, and for that to happen she was forced to meet up with Carter at his mother's place of residence. The same mother

that cursed Novah's name daily. The same woman that swore

Novah trapped her son because of his NFL contract. The same

woman that refused to acknowledge Novah's twin sons until they

were a year old. Even after getting the DNA test done Mrs. Peterson

pretended, they didn't exist.

It burned.

Actually, hurt Novah to the core, but she brushed it off. Mrs.

Peterson didn't have shit on her son. She was ignorant yes, but her

son was next level crazy. Novah knew that with all the madness

Carter brought to her life she could write a book about his ways.

He was the definition of a fuck nigga.

Her phone vibrated in the cup holder grabbing her

attention. Novah picked up the thin but large rose gold device and

smiled.

Normani

Novah's younger sister was the light of her life beside her

twins and their mom. They were as close as siblings could be and

Novah didn't want it to be any other kind of way.

"Hey, what's up?"

Normani sneezed into the phone before clearing her throat.

"Can I borrow a few dollars?" she asked in a chirpy tone.

Novah's smile fell from her pretty round face at her sister's request. Normani not only received inherited pension money from their father's sudden death she also was actively seeing her daughters' father. He was notoriously known throughout the metro Detroit area for being a famous Dj. He worked with the Detroit elite rappers, and he also worked with rappers topping the Billboard charts. With money coming in on a regular Novah felt her sister had no reason to be broke.

Novah frowned as she licked her plump lips.

"Alright, I'll send you some money in a second. I won't preach because I'm not your momma, but this is silly Normani. You should never be broke. We too damn grown for that shit and your little genius ass is too smart for that," she ranted.

Just thinking of Normani walking away from college to be with her now man, made Novah's blood boil. Her sister was so smart it was ridiculous, and Novah felt like it was all going to waste seeing as how she was now out of school and doing nothing with her life.

Her sister smacked her lips as Carters red four-door Camero swooped into the driveway behind her truck. His obnoxiously loud music made her frown deepen. Carter had the audacity to blast his speakers in his ride like he wasn't driving with their kids.

His insensitive ways were always nagging away at Novah's nerves.

"I've had a lot going on this week. My car was down, and I had to pay some extra bills, so I'm broke. Don't be my momma Novah stay in the sister lane. Now thank you for the money in advance, and I love you sugar pie!" Normani replied before ending the call.

Novah sucked her teeth as she sat her phone inside of the cup holder. Like any other sibling, Normani had a way of getting up under her skin.

Novah hit the locks on her truck, and her back door was soon pulled open. The heady scent of Carter's cologne traveled into the truck as he placed their four-year-old son Karter into his car seat. Novah glanced back at her son and smiled wide as she looked him over.

A chance meeting at a popular nightclub in Vegas brought Carter into Novah's life. That had been six years ago, and from there a sexual relationship developed. Novah was a top video model at the time, and Carter had just begun his NFL career. The media went wild with their love story following their every move. The press even brought to the light Carter's extracurricular activities that didn't involve Novah including his affair with the woman that was now his wife. Novah was crushed to learn he had an affair on her but was ready to let it go.

The moment Novah ended things with Carter she learned of her pregnancy.

"Momma!" Karter yelled excitedly.

Novah stared at her handsome son that was the spitting image of his father, and she leaned back to ruffle his curly taper.

"Hey, baby! Mommy missed you so much," she gushed making Karter smile.

He grinned at her before taking a sip of his juice.

Carter chuckled as he strapped in their son King. Even the sound of him doing such a minuscule thing made Novah roll her eyes. The sad thing was that a person that once made her happy was

8

someone she now detested. His cheating had shifted her love to hate, and she didn't see that ever changing. Everything about Carter irritated the hell out of Novah.

"You did? Then I guess that's why you didn't call them all weekend," Carter quipped in a goading manner. He shook his head as he continued ranting. "But you can take your ass to the club and post shit on IG. I'm not getting them kids so you can run the streets. Fuck you think this is? I don't sponsor hoes, ma. You my baby momma so I need for you to carry yourself as such. That partying shit is dead, and you need to have more respect for yourself. I don't need my niggas calling me talking about you in the club dancing with your ass out," Carter spoke angrily.

Novah closed her eyes to calm her racing heart. Somewhere down the line, Carter believed he could dictate her life and often voiced his disdain with how she was living. Novah didn't like it, but instead of arguing with him about the matter she now chose to ignore it. Her mom told her years ago that if you allowed for a fool to behave in an uncivil way, then it was easy to see who the fool was. However, she said if you were to encourage their banter and argue with them that people wouldn't be able to decipher who was who.

Novah followed the guidance of her mom as if her word was law.

Whenever Carter showed his ass, she smiled and kept it moving

making him look dumb as shit in the process.

Novah turned her attention to her son King and ruffled his

curly taper same as she'd done Karter. King was always more alert

than Karter. He watched Novah intently with his light brown eyes

and Novah swallowed hard. She hated the way Carter spoke to her

and prayed his crass attitude didn't rub off on her precious boys.

"I missed you too man. Were you good for daddy?"

King nodded. He smiled at Novah before stretching out in

the seat.

"Sleep," he muttered quietly, and Novah laughed.

"I am as well baby."

Carter snorted at Novah's words.

"Shit, you should be. You been shaking your ass all weekend

instead of being a fucking momma. I would be tired too if I was

you," Carter grumbled before closing King's door.

Novah turned in her seat, and before she could switch gears,

Carter was pulling her door open. He unlatched her seatbelt and grabbed her arm tightly. Novah avoided eye contact with him as she tried to pull away from his grip gently.

"Carter, not tonight and the boys are watching us."

"I'm cool, but I need to holla at you. Come here," he demanded before removing her from the truck.

The sticky warm weather instantly heated Novah's exposed skin. Novah pulled away from Carter as she watched him lustfully eye her shapely body. With the warm May weather heating Michigan, Novah had chosen to wear distressed ankle jeans with a white and cream wrap shirt that exposed her belly and showed off her round bottom. The outfit wasn't revealing only Novah had the type of body that made the simplest attire sexy. She could wear a garbage bag and still garner attention. Her curves weren't something you could cover up.

Carter gave her a deliberate once over choosing to pay close attention to her hips and lower region before peering down into her eyes.

"You look nice," he commented with a sly smirk gracing his face.

His large tattooed hand brazenly cupped his member before he shot her an overconfident smirk. The face that once emanated unspeakable feelings from her heart now made her blood boil. It was crazy how close the line to love and hate was. Novah once loved Carter with every beat of her heart now just the thought of him made her blood pressure rise.

Carter was attractive. That wasn't up for debate. Tall, with a muscular build that was credited to his rigorous workout schedule he had the build to play football and do it well. Carter possessed ebony-hued skin with a handsome square shaped face that had graced many magazine covers. Bedroom eyes and thick lips. He wore his hair in a low fade and sported a trimmed beard. Carter was usually seen in flashy threads with a plethora of chains. He made good money and wanted everyone to know it. The thing was his inner being was ugly, so unattractive that his face, body nor bank account could make up for it.

He was rotten, and if it weren't for the kids, he had a hand in creating Novah would hate him.

"What is this about? What do you want?" she asked wrapping her arms around her body.

Carter let go of the bulge in his grey Phillip Plein joggers and sucked his teeth.

"You don't miss me? I was thinking we could take the kids to Disney next weekend. Do the family thing and shit," he said smiling.

Novah smiled to keep herself from frowning. Her eyes shifted from Carter to the large home that sat in front of them, and she wondered where he went wrong? Had he always been a sucka ass nigga or did something happen in his life to make him that way? It was a known fact his father was a deadbeat, but Carter had strong men in his corner. Like his uncle that had taken on that role as well as his stepdad that had passed a year prior. Carter at least had them when some men had no strong male figures to look up to.

"Would your pregnant wife be there as well with us?" she inquired finally looking up at him.

Carter chuckled at her question. Amusement danced in his lids as he looked Novah over once more. He stepped into Novah's personal space and boldly grabbed her ass. He gripped her meaty cheeks tightly as his warm breath fanned her neck.

"Why the fuck would I take her? We need to make up and stop all this arguing bullshit. It's unhealthy for the kids, and I miss you. It's been way too long since I felt that pussy. Why you acting like you don't miss a nigga?" he asked, and Novah tried to push him back.

His actions and words only irritated her more. She tried to push him again, and he chuckled. It was like shoving a brick wall and expecting it to move. Her small hands did nothing to ease Carter out of her space.

Novah stared up into Carter's dark eyes as she told herself to remain calm. The one thing she was certain that he wanted her to do was step out of her character. Novah simply wouldn't give him the luxury of seeing such a thing.

"That's not going to happen Carter. We've talked about this several times. There is no more us, and there will never be an us again. What we had is over, and we can't ever get it back. Go home to your pregnant wife," she said calmly.

"Yes, please do so before she ruins the good things that you do have in your life," Mrs. Peterson interjected walking up.

Carter quickly stepped back and covered his growing

erection. Novah looked past him at his mother and cleared her

throat.

"Mrs. Peterson," she spoke politely.

Mrs. Peterson clad in her floral silk nightgown and royal

blue housecoat rolled her deep brown eyes. Her disdain for Novah

showed on her gracefully aging face as she stared Novah's way.

"The minute he brought you home I knew your little stuck

up ass would be a problem. You're too pretty. I always told him

about shallow, gold digging ass hussies like you, and his silly self still

fell victim to you. Even had them boys by you like you could

change. You're all about yourself, and you always will be little girl.

Now have some dignity about yourself. He's a married man with a

child on the way. He didn't choose you Novah. He could have, but

he didn't. Accept that and respect his marriage. God will not bless

you with another woman's husband child. Now, are you going to

agree to the pay cut?"

Novah's lips pressed into a thin line as she glared at Carter's

mom. She envisioned herself slapping the bob style wig from her

head then shoving it into her big ass mouth.

15

Carter chuckled lowly as he pulled on his mothers' arm.

"Momma chill out with all that. No matter what Novah gone be a part of this family, and you know that. She knows I'm with Mel and that ain't ever changing. Let me holla at Novah real quick though. Everything's all good," he said with a shit eating grin on his face and attempted to turn his mother around.

Mrs. Peterson nodded while giving Novah a stern look. Novah stared at Carter's mom wondering why she'd never liked her from the start but had instantly taken a liking to his wife, Mel. The only answer she could come up with was that even though their age gap was huge, his mom was jealous of her. It was like Normani had told her on numerous occasions.

Old bitches hate too.

"Remember that he's married now. Twins or not you are not his wife," Mrs. Peterson told Novah before walking off.

Novah's small hands clenched into fists as she watched Carter lead his mother back into the home. For as long as she could remember she'd taken Mrs. Peterson's verbal lashings, but it had gotten old. Mrs. Peterson knew why she wasn't with Carter, and she also knew the truth. If Novah wanted to, she could be Carters wife and the woman carrying his next child. However, she didn't, and that was why he was with his backup plan instead. Benchwarmer, seat filler or bed warmer. There were many ways to call Mel a fool but it all boiled down to her being the one woman that was willing to take all the shit Carter threw her way just so she could call him her man.

The one dumb ass woman that was stupid enough to stick around.

"I'ma end up hurting that old bitch," Novah grumbled wishing she could push her niceness to the side to let Mrs. Peterson know about herself.

Carter jogged back over to the truck as Novah frowned. Still crossed about his mother's hateful, ignorant, and clueless words Novah glared up at him.

"What do you need to talk to me about? I didn't come over here for this bullshit."

Carter caressed her cheek tenderly before rubbing her arm. His actions was one of a lover, but Novah knew better. She pushed his hand away, and he cleared his throat. He seemed to be upset with her like she'd been the one to wrong him in some way.

"Stop doing that shit, and you know how she gets at times. She's upset that we didn't work out. Hell, I am too, but it's like this. I got hit with some suspensions because I tested dirty for coke. I'm not addicted to crack or nothing crazy like that. A nigga had a good night, and they caught me slipping. I been paying fines all year and shit is getting tight now that Melanie is pregnant. I wanna see if we can cut down the child support and to help you out, I will start keeping them half the week," Carter replied talking quickly.

Something he often did when he was lying or nervous.

Novah shook her head not having to think about his question. Melanie hated her and her twins. Novah hated that they had to go over there for the two days on the weekend that they did. There was no way in hell she was going to allow for him to keep her babies for half the week. So far Melanie hadn't done anything spiteful to them, but Novah didn't want to chance it.

She knew that a bitter heart could lead a person to do unspeakable things. Carter was the prime example of that. He'd gone from treating her like his queen and proclaiming his love for her to calling her every degrading name imaginable while bashing her character.

18

"I'm sorry but I can't. They come over on the weekend, and that's enough. I can't see me giving you half a week because of your issues with work. The answer is no Carter. Sorry."

She offered him half a shrug as he stared down at her. Novah turned to get in her truck and Carter grabbed her arm jerking her back.

"Damn so you can't even work with a nigga? Your gold-digging ass is about to piss me the fuck off," he snapped angrily.

The growl in his deep voice alerted Novah to his displeasure with her answer; still, she couldn't budge. It wasn't about the money. She preferred to have her sons in her care. Carter was rarely home, and she didn't feel comfortable with a woman that didn't like her raising her kids.

"Melanie hates our sons and me. In case you didn't know that she does Carter. I'm not agreeing to that and let's be real you are far from broke. You were just in Europe last week, and you bought Melanie that new house out in Troy. If money is tight for you, then I suggest you downgrade. Maybe even sell some of the things you have to catch up on bills. My sons are already getting the bare minimum from you."

Carter's nostrils flared as he glared down at Novah. His hands balled into fists, and he slowly nodded. Of course, to him, she was once again the bad guy, but she didn't care. He'd been the one to drop dirty. Why should she have to pay for it? Carter made millions from the NFL, and somehow, he'd managed to give her only $12,000 in child support per child. She knew women that got three times that amount, yet she never complained. To keep the peace, she made do with the money and often paid for extra things out of her account. Novah couldn't see herself taking less than that when the man before her spent money like it was going out of style.

Her kids wouldn't suffer because he'd fucked up.

"Damn it's like that?" he asked breaking the silence.

Novah sighed wishing she'd never had to see him that day. Any interaction with him was a fucking headache.

"Carter you messed up now deal with it. Yes, I own that spa, but I still have bills to pay. I can't take a loss because of you. Your sons deserve a good life as well. Don't they?"

Carter took a step towards Novah that made her back up into her truck. The cold, menacing stare he gave her was making her heart race. He'd never struck her before, but it was something that she wouldn't put past him.

His head cocked to the side as he stared down at her.

"Didn't I just fucking say I would take them for half of the week? You pretty as shit but you need to be smart as well. You sounding real fucking dumb right now. Mel would never hurt our kids. I would break her fucking neck if she ever did some shit like that. I need you to do this for me. Come on Novah," he pleaded.

Novah broke his gaze and slowly shook her head. If she didn't stand for something, Carter would try to make her fall for anything. When it came to her sons and their wellbeing, she would never budge.

"Carter the answer is no. Can you move?"

Carter's enraged eyes bored into Novah as he nodded slowly. He bit down so hard on his bottom lip that Novah wondered if he would puncture it with his teeth. She watched him mumble something inaudible before swallowing hard.

"Fuck you then bitch. You'll be seeing me in court with your trashy ass. Once they see how you hoe around instead of raising our sons, they'll grant me split custody," he spat venomously.

Novah ignored his spiteful words and quickly climbed into her truck. As she switched gears, Carter began to kick her door. Novah glanced into the backseat at her sons before glaring over at Carter. His thick brows were pulled together as he kicked the truck one last time.

It was enough to make the expensive ride shake.

"I hate him. I fucking hate him," she murmured feeling her eyes water with tears.

Novah shared a staring match with Carter until he cracked a smile. He chuckled as he walked away. Novah watched him reverse out of his mother's driveway and speed at an alarming rate down the residential street. Her eyes shot to the back of the truck once more, and she noticed Karter was still asleep. King, however, wasn't and the stare he placed on her was enough to make a teardrop from her hooded eyes.

"It's okay baby," she said soothingly.

King nodded, and gradually his eyes lowered. Sleep overcame him as she reversed out of the driveway and headed home.

The colonial-style cottage house smelled of soul food mixed with her mother's favorite candles for the moment. Her sons jetted off in the large home in search of their playroom as she stepped out of her leather designer slides. Novah sat her keys on the ring like she was still a member of the house before heading towards the kitchen.

"Ugh! Why the hell did you and your greedy sons come over? Maybe I wanted my momma to myself for once," Normani quipped stepping out of the family room.

Novah rolled her eyes as she flipped her baby sister off. She was two days shy of seeing Carter and was still in a funk. Not to mention she'd woken up with a deep ache in her sex that only a thick penis could satisfy. It also didn't help that she had another money request from her sister.

"Stop it. I was her first born so I will always be a regular in this home. Me and momma have a bond that your spoiled ass won't understand. It's no secret that you were the oops baby Normani.

You're simply here by luck sugar. I'm guessing it was one of those drunk nights when daddy had too much Hennessey and forgot to strap up," Novah jested.

Normani's jaw fell slack at Novah's words as she trailed behind her. Much like she did when they were younger.

"Ouch. No lie that was rude as hell of you to say and I see you in a mood today. Did you get my money request and if so, why didn't you accept it, Grinch?"

Novah snorted before she stopped walking to turn to her sister. The woman that stared back at her looked pretty per usual. Whereas Novah was naturally thick with mahogany shaded skin Normani was slim thick with a rich chocolate brown skin tone. Normani possessed a natural shine to her flawless skin and was always sporting a bright smile. Even when she was upset, she found a reason to show off her sunken in dimples and Novah admired that about her younger sister.

Novah inspected her sister quickly admiring her pastel pink pleated high waisted shorts that she'd paired with a blue collard top and the matching shorts jacket. Normani was the perfect example of not judging a book by the cover because her style was opposite of her looks. Like Novah she could star in any video or clothing campaign, but Normani was insanely smart and dressed like she belonged on the set of The Big Bang Theory. Novah was worried her sister would get bullied at a younger age for her unique style, but instead, people embraced it and Novah was grateful for that. She'd undoubtedly beat anyone's ass for ragging on her baby sister.

She sighed as she stared into Normani's hazel eyes. Normani was so much more than just a mother and Novah wished that she could see that.

"If you would have stayed in school you would be in your fourth year Normani. Close as hell to getting your degree and not worrying about money. You do know that if you don't work, you don't eat right?" Novah questioned with raised brows.

Normani stared at Novah with pursed lips.

"I don't have time for school right now because if I did, I would be there. I have a job, and that's being a mother. The hardest job on the planet might I add. Things with Tru have been all over the place lately. I caught him talking to this negligible ass singer, and I lost it. I can admit I took things too far by showing up at the studio and attacking him, but I knew in my heart that he was flirting with that bitch. I know Tru, and his friendly ass was doing the most so I had to show him that it wouldn't be tolerated."

Novah nodded wanting her sister to get to the point. Unfortunately, this was a story she was used to hearing from her. Tru started out as the ideal man for Normani, but Novah had always had a bad feeling about him. It was all in the sneaky ass grin he wore on his face.

"Okay, and you did what after jumping on him because we all know you like to go crazy when you're mad?"

Normani sighed. Regret flashed briefly across her face, but it only made Novah roll her eyes. Normani had more than a few screws missing when it came to how she reacted to Tru's sneaky ways.

Normani smoothed out the few wrinkles in her shorts as she cleared her throat.

"I put his phone in River's soiled diaper. I then wiped the rest of the feces across some of his clothing. He's full of shit so I assumed he would like to smell like it as well," Normani replied calmly.

Novah smiled as she turned back around.

"And let me guess he went ghost on you with the money again? His way of teaching you a lesson, huh?"

"Yep and now she thinks I'm supposed to give her some of mine. I keep telling that child of mine to go back to school. I worked hard for my money. Went to college for over eight years. Put my blood sweat and tears into becoming who I am. I won't hand out money to my grown ass daughter simply because she can't go work for her own," Diana said as they entered into the large kitchen.

Normani groaned as Novah made her way over to her mom. Diana was everything Novah felt a mother should be. Strong, beautiful, and kind-hearted. Diana owned her own doctor's office that specialized in women gynecology. Diana was accredited and widely known as one of the best doctors in Michigan. She'd also given birth to her grandchildren. She didn't trust anyone else with her lovebugs that she affectionately called them, but her.

"I know that's right ma. Let your lazy daughter know," Novah retorted, and Normani discreetly flipped her off. "And she's sticking her middle finger up at me and everything," she snitched.

Normani rolled her eyes at Novah as Diana glanced over at her.

27

"Oh really? Don't wanna work and you have bad manners.

Who raised you?"

Normani and Novah laughed at their mother's playfulness.

Diana carried her age well and always told her girls it was because of

the way she took care of her body. She drank plenty of water

worked out weekly and loved the Lord. Diana said with that

regimen you couldn't go wrong.

"You did! You raised me doctor Diana. It's because of you

and daddy that I'm like this and I have a job. I'm a mother. Why is

it that you all keep saying that like its nugatory?" Normani asked.

Diana waved her off while Novah snickered.

"Well, I don't even know what that means so mom you can

answer that question for the both of us."

Novah's mom laughed at her response.

"Just another way to say unimportant. And nobody is

downplaying you being a mom Normani. I had two kids, and I still

went to college. Your father and I worked hard and gave you all that

we didn't have, but now our work is done. If you were down and out

than momma would be there for you. Hell lets be real for any

reason I will be there for you, but I also have to give you tough love when it's needed. You're twenty-one with a child. Do something

with your life Normani because what you're doing isn't working.

Your whole life you've been above average, yet you've allowed for

Tru's nappy headed ass to bring you down to this regular level, and

I have to say it doesn't look good on you sweetie."

Diana stopped talking to smile at Normani.

"I want to see you walk across that stage. You told me it was

your dream to be a software engineer and you were on your way to

becoming that. With your smarts, I know you can finish early. All

you have to do is go back, and I won't let up on you until you do.

River is a blessing, but that shouldn't stop you from getting your

degree. You should use that even more as motivation to finish

school."

"You all just don't understand," Normani shook her head

with a frown marring her pretty face.

"It's not about us, not understanding. You're in love, and we

get it. I promise you, baby, we've both felt those feelings. You're

invested in your family, and that's great but is he invested in you?

He spoon feeds you money and is constantly being caught in a lie.

You've changed your whole life for him. I've watched you help him

29

chase his dreams while pushing back your own and I'm supposed to welcome that negro into my home? I can't and I won't. You don't even put Normani first so why should he?" their mom asked Normani.

Normani shrugged with sad eyes and Diana sighed.

"Its fine baby, the Lord will get you together. Since you've left school, I've been praying that you find your way back and you will. It might not even be college, but you'll find your purpose. I believe it," she said in a sweeter voice making Normani smile.

Novah nodded agreeing with her mother wholeheartedly while looking over a blog post that her cousin had just sent to her. Novah's breathing grew ragged as she read the headline for the article.

NFL star Carter Wilson is soon to be in court for split custody of his twins! Word has it his baby momma ex-video model turned spa owner Novah Royale is asking for more money!

Novah's hand shook as she scrolled down to the bottom of the page to read the comments.

Sheacutered81: she a gold digger anyway that fucked all the rappers. I heard she was Kasam's side bitch for years.

Lilmam02: she cute but I know he regrets hitting that shit raw now.

RandyMK: she bad, I'd still hit that.

Lina: these niggas gone get enough of fucking these plastic body bitches. Now he gotta pay up, and I don't feel bad for him. She ain't all that anyway.

Novah swallowed hard as she sat her phone down. It was one thing to have people speak on you that knew but for people that didn't know a thing about you, talk down on you like you was nothing was the worst. Novah briefly considered replying before shaking it off. Seconds later her sister picked the device up and read over the short article. The crazy thing was it was only a few short words, but everything the writer said was facts. Carter was taking her to court, but it wasn't for money. It was for his own selfish gain.

A true characteristic of a fuck nigga.

"Wow, who keeps sending them your damn business? It has to be someone from his family," Normani mumbled reading the article for a second time.

"Mouth Normani. I am not one of your girls and forget those blogs Novah if that's what that mess is. You did the right thing by saying no. That negro is making good money. Don't let his woe is me story get to you," Diana said to Novah.

Novah nodded with low tinted eyes. She placed her elbows onto the countertop, and her head hung low. Her sad disposition was enough for Normani to soothingly rub her back. Novah didn't want to cry but couldn't help it.

She was so fucking tired of fighting with Carter.

"I'm just over it momma. The pipes at my spa busted, so I have to get them fixed. My roof at my house is messed up so it's looking like I will have to replace that soon and I'm starting to get overwhelmed. I'm so tired of doing all of this by myself then to have to use energy I don't have to fight him is killing me. Sometimes I just want to give up," Novah shamefully admitted.

Diana nodded while pulling her turkey from out of the oven.

"What does momma say do when the going gets too tough?"

"Pray," Normani responded still rubbing Novah's back.

"And I say it because I mean it. We're women baby. We are able to withstand anything that's thrown our way. You can't give up.

32

You have boys that are looking up to you. Boys that are looking

forward to seeing your face every day. I know you're tired and I

know you're hurting, but this mess with Carter can't bring you down.

That's what he wants, but it's not happening. You're a Royale, and

more importantly, your father is the Most High. With him, by your

side, you can do anything. Even go up against someone as evil as

Carter. I'll call the lawyer and make sure he's on his job. Carter isn't

cutting that money. Hell, I'll be on his bitter momma's doorsteps if I

have to be to make sure he knows what's up," her mother replied.

Novah swallowed hard and looked up at her mom.

"But he has more money than me, and the media loves him.

What makes you think I could win a case against him?" she asked.

Diana stirred her greens before responding.

"Because when you have an evil heart, you can only get away

with your scandalous ways for so long. Stop looking so down and

help me finish up this food so we can eat. Carter can't steal any of

the joy we have over here. Let's not even discuss his ugly ass

anymore," Diana replied making Novah smile.

Even if it were only for the moment, Novah would ignore his threats and pretend he didn't exist. With him out of the picture, her life didn't seem bad at all.

Novah held the coffee cup tightly as her eyes skated around her back room. The contractor stood by her closely as she inspected his work.

"Bueno?"

Novah nodded. She glanced over at Jorge and smiled. He always took care of her and because he'd known her late father it was at a discounted rate. She adored him much more for that.

"Si perfecto, espero que esta sea la ultima vez que me veas este ano."

Jorge laughed while pulling out his car keys.

"Rezo que sea," he replied before flashing her a parting smile.

Novah took one last sip of her coffee before sitting it down. As she started up the kiosk at the front desk her front doors chimed. Her eyes peered up, and her breath got caught in her throat. Novah's heart thundered in her chest as the insanely attractive russet-hued male swaggered her way.

He adjusted the diamond link chain adorning his neck before gazing down at her. The clothing he was draped in was eye-catching and only added to his sexiness. The tattered blue jeans that he wore an army green camo style BAPE shirt with suited his tall frame. On his head was a pink El Chapo fitted cap and even that looked sexy on the handsome guy. Subtle jewelry caught her eye as it sparkled from the light glares that hit it in the room, but his face was the star of the show. He possessed the kind of face that you couldn't help but stare at.

"How you doing?"

Novah smiled. His lips were full and evenly colored. His eyes were down casted and dreamy. The kind of eyes you would want to wake up to in the morning.

"Excuse me you good?"

Novah's brows drew together as she realized she was

tripping, and she laughed to play off her nervousness. She shook

her head and the handsome, tall man that smelled of everything she

didn't need but craved at the moment smirked down at her.

"I'm Durand. I was looking to book a spa party for my mom

and her girls. Can I do that?" he inquired.

Novah glanced behind him and noticed the door was

cracked. Something she would fix as soon as he left. She peered

back up at Durand, and his face mixed with his name lit a bulb

inside of her head.

"From the rap group, Luca Gang?"

Durand nodded coolly. He dipped his head, and she

watched him roam his brown orbs over her curvy frame. Novah

wore a black ribbed strapless dress with Chanel sneakers and a blue

jean top that was tied around her waist. She smoothed a hand over

her two-day-old body wave curls, and Durand smiled at her.

His thick lips parted, and his tongue swiped against his lower

lip as he gazed her way.

"Yeah that's me but can you do that? I didn't know you wasn't open. The door was cracked," he said with his eyes roaming around the spa.

Novah followed his line of sight and took in her partially cluttered space. The front of her business was black and white themed. Novah loved the colors and often filled her home and establishment with it. The walls were a stark white while the floor was a checkered black and shiny white tile that people often raved over. On the front walls were uplifting word art canvas's in bold graffiti text by a popular Detroit designer that now resided in Philly. Novah had flown out to New York to purchase the exotic art prints and four months in she was still in awe of the artwork.

A small seating area filled with plush black loveseats and a glass table sat in the area to the left of the room while drinking supplies mixed with magazines and glass shelves filled with nail polishes sat on the left wall. Novah stared at the large wall of polishes lost in her thoughts until Durand cleared his throat.

Novah nodded forcing herself to look back at the handsome man before her. Durand had her temporarily discombobulated. Things that usually came second nature to her was on brief pause.

"I'm actually closed right now, but I will be opening up back soon..." Novah stopped talking and shook her head. "What I meant to say was that I will be opening back up soon. I can give you a birthday party reserve sheet, and we can go from there," she replied trying to pull herself together.

Durand nodded instead of verbally responding and Novah moved fast to grab him the form that he needed to fill out.

Thirty minutes later Novah had Durand booked, and his mother was all set to go. Durand pulled his fob out of his pocket as Novah grabbed her blogger bag style crossbody from her front desk. He looked her over as she placed on her items and she stared up at him shyly.

"Did you need anything else?"

Durand looked at her intently for a few moments before chuckling.

"Nah, you have a good day ma," he replied before walking out of the building.

As the door closed leaving in Durand's wake, his scent Novah was able to relax. She sighed with relief, and when light gas filtered from between her fat butt cheeks, she laughed.

"He was so damn fine he had me holding everything in," she commented.

Novah shut down her spa and headed to her truck that sat in the reserved parking spot. A handsome dark-skinned man approached her with a sly smirk on his round face.

Damn two fine ass men in one day.

"How you doing beautiful?" he asked as she hit the locks on the truck.

Novah stopped walking and looked the man over before smiling. He was dressed clean in a two-piece grey suit that appeared to be custom made. His face was insanely attractive as he gave off a young Morris Chestnut circa The Best Man vibes, but after seeing Durand, the man paled in comparison.

"I'm fine. Do I know you?"

The man frowned and licked his lips. His slanted eyes looked Novah over as he sighed.

"I'm not sure. Are you Novah Royale?" he asked coolly.

Novah nodded, and he grinned down at her. The man swiftly pulled a white paper from inside of his suit jacket and walked up on her.

"Ms. Royale, you've been served," he said passing her the paper.

Novah's heart raced as she looked down at the papers.

Carter was taking her to court, and he wasn't requesting split custody. Instead, he was seeking full custody of their twins. Her knees grew week, and she found herself immediately growing ill.

"You okay?" the process server asked watching her.

Novah waved him off as she composed herself. She closed her eyes and thought of her boys. Yes, Carter loved them but not like her. Everything that she did was for the betterment of her sons. They was her life, and now he wanted to take them all away because of his own fuck up. It wasn't even because he wanted them.

Novah's rage grew to dangerous levels, and she hopped in her truck and called up her sorry ass baby daddy.

Carter ended the call and hit her back on a video call.

"I hate him," she muttered answering the call.

Carter's wife Melanie sat on a large plush king-sized bed with a cheshire grin on her thin brown face. Melanie was pretty in a plain jane sort of way. She wasn't Carter's type that Novah knew for sure, but she worshipped the ground Carter walked on and the way that

fed his ego was enough for him to keep her around.

Melanie licked her thin lips and pushed some of her

shoulder-length hair away from her face as she grinned at Novah.

"My husband is downstairs with the boys. I take it you were

served today. I hope you're happy now. All you had to do was take

the pay cut. Are you that money hungry Novah that you couldn't do

that?" she asked.

Novah opened her mouth and quickly clamped her lips

shut. If she started to go off, she was certain she wouldn't stop.

"Tell him to call me," she replied and gave Melanie a big

smile before hanging up.

Seconds later a text came through to her phone from

Carter's cell that made her want to beat some ass.

Once we get the kids, then you'll have nothing. No child

support, no boys and finally no more of my man's time. Now that's

something I have been praying for!

Novah closed out the text with a heavy heart. She wanted to

call her family and friends and vent to them but opted out of doing

so. Her anger and pain from dealing with Carter and his ditzy ass

41

wife was so great she chose to stew in it alone. Her next move had to

be her best move because her children's home front was on the line.

2

#newme

Her long dark ashe blonde strands swept past her shoulders and hung loosely down her back as she stood confidently before the people. To them she was sure they thought she was putting on a front, but she wasn't. Even on her worse days, she slayed. Billie had been blessed with impeccable genes. Beauty flowed through her effortlessly. Even when in distress she looked nothing short of gorgeous.

Like now as she remembered the darkest time of her life, she came off stunning. She wore blue ankle jeans that were distressed with a sleeveless Black Gyrl Magic, top made by her friend, a Detroit based stylist from her new t-shirt line. Billie paired the look with Jonatina style Christian Louboutin heels and gold

David Yurman bangles that were a gift from her man.

Billie's chocolate colored eyes peered at the people intently

watching her, and she licked her lips.

"Hi, my name is Bethany, but I hate that name, so I go by

Billie instead," her soft voice said, and a few people laughed. Billie

shot them a playful smirk before continuing. "I've been sober for

seven hundred and thirty days. Tomorrow is the anniversary of the

day that I ran my vehicle into oncoming traffic while my twelve-

month-old son slept in the back seat. It hurts to admit this, but all

that day I'd been getting drunk. I was out hanging with my friends,

and I partied hard. So hard that I almost forgot to pick up my baby,

but I didn't. As I headed home, I blacked out. I ran into a minivan,

and from there a four-car pileup happened. We should have died,

but God had a plan for me that was greater than the one I had for

myself. He wanted me to live. He wanted my son to live as well. To

serve out his purpose and I'm so grateful to him for that. Without

this facility that wouldn't be possible. I'm not perfect. I wanted to

drink yesterday when I thought about the fact that I couldn't put my

son to bed because of my reckless behavior, but I didn't. If I would have picked that bottle up that would have been the worst thing for me. I would have been right back at step one. I owe my son so much more than a drunk mother. I wanna sponsor one of you so if you feel like I could be a good ear or shoulder to cry on find me after this is over with," Billie said before sitting down.

Billie looked on as three more people stood and began to tell their testimony. They were in an Alcoholics Anonymous meeting not a church, but Billie very much considered them testimonies. Her story alone was powerful and showed God's grace. Despite being an alcoholic, she was still alive and slowly changing her ways.

In a matter of three years, she ruined her modeling career and lost custody of her son all because of her addiction to liquor. Billie had partaken in ecstasy occasionally, but alcohol was the one vice she couldn't give up until she had no choice but to. It was either liquor or her life, and Billie chose herself. She had to or else she was sure death would be coming much sooner for her.

"You've come such a long way," Mr. Carmichael said walking up.

He was the first-person Billie met when she'd started her AAA meetings. He was an older gentleman that had lost years of his life to liquor. He was also devoting the rest of his life to helping as many alcoholics that he could.

Billie smiled as she peered up at him. She slowly stood and tugged down her top that was committed to rising up. She gave Mr. Carmichael a quick hug before stepping back.

"And I've got such a long way to go. I'll look at my calendars and see the days I've done, but it doesn't make me proud. I still feel the shame," Billie spoke earnestly before looking away.

Mr. Carmichael nodded with an empathetic gaze on her.

"Honey beating yourself up about this will only get you back to the bottle. The devil will make you think you haven't changed because you are changing, and he doesn't want that. If you were going down the wrong path, then he wouldn't be messing with you. How is your son?"

Billie thought of her small son Kawan and smiled. He was the best thing to ever happen to her.

"He's good. With his father right now. I'm praying for the day that I can get him back, you know?"

Mr. Carmichael nodded. He rubbed her arm gently before placing his hands in his cream-colored pants pockets.

"And you will. The courts will see how much you've changed. Just keep up the good work," he said speaking words of encouragement like always before walking off.

Billie headed for the door when a small tawny brown hand grabbed her arm. Billie glanced back at the pretty young lady, and she smiled.

"Hi, I'm Billie," Billie spoke politely.

The girl let her hand go and hugged herself. Her slanted dark eyes shifted nervously around the room before peering up at Billie who had on her at least four inches.

"I um..." the girl stopped speaking and cleared her throat. She straightened her back, and Billie smiled.

"Yes, no matter what be strong with it," Billie said quietly.

"This is different for me. My parents are making me come. If I don't, they said they're going to cut off my money, and I'm a full-time college student so I can't have that. I don't have time for a job. My name is Charisse, but everyone calls me Reese," she replied.

47

Billie nodded. She noted how tiny the girl was with her pretty round face and wide-set brown eyes. Reese wore long box braids that hung to her waist with fitted clothes and a timid smile.

"Nice to meet you, Reese. Are your parents the only reason why you're here?" she asked.

Reese's eyes fell, and she stared down at the ground. She kicked small dirt around the floor as her shoulders sagged.

"I kind of picked up a drinking habit once I started school. A few months back I had to get my stomach pumped, and since then my parents have been tripping out on me. Like I can't control it," she quipped with an eye roll.

Billie cleared her throat. Her eyes cast down to her Apple watch before she looked back to the small Reese.

"Take my number down. I would love to sponsor you, but first, we need to discuss some things. Call me tomorrow so we can set up a time to get together," Billie told her.

Reese's head shot up, and she quickly whipped out her silver cellular device. Billie called off her number before exiting the building. In front of it double parked like always was her boyfriend of two years Dreux. Billie's face stretched into a wide smile. Her feet moved at a swift pace as she headed for Dreux's white 7 series BMW.

Billie slid inside of the sleek vehicle and only as his audacious cologne assaulted her senses was, she able to relax. His large hand fell onto her small thigh as he pulled away.

Billie's eyes ventured down to the tattoo of the queen chess peace adorning his hand, and her heart swelled. He always told her she was his queen. His ace in the hole. The one person he would stop the world from spinning for, and she believed him.

Dreux breathed life into Billie when she was ready to give up. He loved her at her lowest, and for that, she would always love him with everything that she had in her.

"You good, baby?"

The deep timber in his voice made her vaginal muscles clench together. Billie didn't think anyone was more in love than she was. Dreux made her so happy she felt as if she were floating on a cloud whenever she was in his presence.

"Yes, just tired. Every time I speak about my past and how bad I messed up it does something to me. It's the reason I lost

Kawan, and it kills me," she admitted sadly with her eyes still trained on his tattoo.

The shading and attention to detail the artist placed on the artwork was amazing to Billie.

"But that's old shit, and it doesn't help that you keep dwelling on it. The things we've done in our past doesn't define who we are. Of course, a child killer or rapist can't come back from that, but God has the final say so, and only he can judge us. Life is about progression. I watched you suffer and go through rehab. That shit wasn't easy, and I could see that you wanted to give up plenty of times, but you didn't. Give yourself credit for that. Malachi not giving you no problems, is he?" he asked.

The tone of his voice told her that if she were to say yes nothing good would come from it. Billie shook her head while staring his way.

"He isn't," her light voice answered quietly.

Dreux stared over at her for a moment before continuing.

"You fucked up. We all know that but shit so has everybody else. Your mishap was just bigger than some peoples and its some niggas that fucked up way more than you did. Stop living in the past baby. It will only hold you back. Focus on all the good you have now and keep it moving. You changed for the better and don't let nobody make you feel otherwise ma. I don't know a woman alive besides my mom that is as strong as you are and I'll fuck up anybody that has some negative shit to say about you," he told her.

His words brought a big smile to Billie's face. Billie pulled out her cellphone to check her text messages, and the smile Dreux had just given her was wiped away by her son's father, Malachi.

Kawan was calling to hear your voice, and you couldn't even pick the phone up. You with some nigga or out drinking? Which one is it this time? Drunk ass.

Billie cleared her throat as she erased his message. She called up Malachi and lowered the volume on her phone as she waited for him to take the call.

"What?"

Malachi's tone dripped with anger. Billie knew of his disgust with her but felt it was unwarranted. If Billie were to be with Malachi, she was sure she'd see a friendlier side of him, but he wasn't the man she wanted. What they had couldn't dare compare to what she now had with Dreux.

What she ever had with Dreux and Malachi had never been

an option for Billie. He knew that, and deep-down Billie felt that

was also the reason why he was mad. Malachi assumed their son

would bond them together, but even Kawan couldn't make Billie be

with a man she felt nothing for.

"I got your message, and that wasn't the case Malachi. I was

in my meeting. Today was my anniversary. Two years clean."

Malachi clapped loudly into the phone.

"You want some kind of fucking reward for that? You

should be clean. Your ass should have never been drunk in the first

fucking place! Fuck I'ma congratulate you for on some shit you

should be doing? When your son that you don't fucking take care of

call you, you better fucking answer. At least act like you love him

with your smutty ass," he replied snidely before ending the call.

Billie's heart pounded as she lowered the phone and placed

it in her clutch. Dreux stopped at the red light and glanced over at

her. Billie chose to gaze out of the window instead of staring back at

her man.

With just one look he would know that the call hadn't gone

well.

"Who was that?"

Billie swallowed hard.

"That was Malachi. Kawan wanted to talk, and I was in the meeting. He said that Kawan got upset," she partially lied.

Dreux licked his lips.

"He's a kid, and they do that sometimes. He'll be good. How Malachi been doing on that co-parenting shit?" Dreux asked.

Billie swallowed down her pain to turn to her man. Her eyes soaked in his handsome appearance. Looking relaxed as ever in his black crew neck designer tee that he'd paired with Balmain jeans and black Buscemi kicks he looked sexy like always. Dreux had the creamiest tawny brown skin she'd ever seen on a man. It was like it was melted onto his body. The perfect brown she always mused. Dreux was tall with a baller build to him. Toned muscles, chiseled jaw, and full lips. Thick brows with a curly taper and to finish up his look, he rocked a trimmed beard. Nothing outrageous but enough hair to make your panties go moist. The letter B with a crown hanging off the side of it was tattooed on his neck, and Billie often found herself licking it while riding his big member.

Dreux was the shit on any day of the week, and Billie was all too glad to call him her own. He could have turned to the streets like his older brother Donny but instead went the safer route. Dreux worked two jobs while in college and boosted his credit score up enough to start his own shipping company. He had two warehouses and was working on a third one.

"Yes, I just need him back home with me baby. I miss my son so much," she said like he didn't know.

Dreux drove off and squeezed her thigh gently.

"I know baby, and you will get him back. I keep telling you to let me know if you want me to holla at that nigga."

Billie quickly shook her head. That was the last thing she needed for Dreux to do.

"No, but thanks for offering. I'm just going to bide my time. I was offered to do two jobs in New York next week, and I could use the money so of course, I said yes. I would love for you to come with me. Would you?"

Dreux chuckled.

"You already know the answer to that baby. Of course, I will. I wanted to scout out a building out in Patterson anyway, so that's right on time. But check it, I need for you to close your eyes for me real quick," he replied.

Billie grinned at him, and he shot her a cocky smirk. He licked his lips, and she sighed.

"And what do I get if I play along?"

Dreux shrugged, his eyes briefly glanced at her before turning back to the road.

"You get me sucking on that pussy all night long now close 'em," he replied making her giggle.

Billie shut her eyes and bounced her leg nervously as she rode with Dreux. Thirty minutes later Dreux pulled up to the luxurious DeLoines Hotel. If you ever heard of the Ritz, the Hilton then you should have heard of the DeLoines. It was one of the few black five-star hotels in the states, and the first one ever was in Michigan.

Billie glanced out of the window as he pulled up to valet and Dreux pinched her thigh.

"I didn't say open them pretty ass eyes ma," he playfully scolded her.

Billie smiled. She glanced over at her man and stared into his eyes.

"What's this?"

Dreux tossed his car into park and cleared his throat.

"It's your anniversary, and I'm very fucking proud of you. This is your man showing you that. Come on. The night is just getting started," he replied.

Excitement surged through Billie as she quickly exited the car. She clung onto Dreux as they entered the hotel after grabbing a valet ticket.

Instead of going upstairs to the room Dreux took Billie into one of the three five-star restaurants inside of the hotel. They were quickly seated, and as Billie read over the menu, Dreux slid a green box across the table. Billie's eyes landed on the logo, and she smiled.

"You spoil me," she gushed quietly.

She opened the box as Dreux gazed her way.

"I don't spoil you enough. You like it?"

Billie snorted. The diamonds dancing on the Rolex was

enough to make her heart momentarily stop beating. Did she like it?

Shit, she loved it. What woman didn't like nice things?

Billie tenderly ran her finger over the expensive watch and

looked up at her man. She could still vividly remember the day

she'd met him inside of the Somerset Collections Mall. They were

both so young back then, but even then, she'd been smitten with his

fifteen-year-old self. Dreux was unlike any man she'd ever come

across.

He'd placed her in the friend zone fearing she was too

snooty for him, but Billie quickly showed him that she was a down

to earth kind of girl. Her looks often intimidated men and Dreux

hadn't been exempt from that. They became best friends and stuck

to each other like glue until prom night.

Prom night changed everything for both of them.

"I love it. Thank you," she finally responded.

Dreux nodded. He licked his lips and brushed his hand over

that curly ass taper that she loved so much. They ordered shortly

after and Dreux was then putting on her new watch.

"I got a big ass contract with the DeLoines the other day. I didn't say shit because I wasn't sure if it would go through, but it did. They now use my company for all their business needs in Michigan, so that's more fucking money for us. I had to lace you with some gifts. I come up then we come up. You know, that right?"

His voice, his words always placed her in a spell. An you're one *lucky* ass woman spell that she prayed she never woke up from.

Billie nodded while staring into his eyes. Dreux leaned over the table and pecked her lips while keeping eye contact. His tongue sucked on her bottom lip, and she giggled. She thought of the dark times that she faced while he was away and was relieved that they were over. Those were some of the roughest days of her life. Hell, they'd even forced her to do things like fall off into bed with Malachi.

A mistake that she regretted but didn't hate because it had brought her Kawan. Her biggest blessing.

"I know and wow. I'm so proud of you. Everything that you said you would do you did."

Dreux chuckled.

58

"Shit, real niggas do real things. For you and my mom's, I couldn't fail. Hell, I won't," he promised as their drinks were brought to the table.

A throat cleared in the back of the room and Billie's eyes widened. She had been so caught up in Dreux that she hadn't noticed there was a stage along with a small band. As the band sat down and prepared to play a local artist that was making waves in the music industry stepped onto the center of the stage. Her name was Naiyana, and she was outlandishly gorgeous. She not only had a voice that was being compared to Lauryn Hill she had vitiligo and was embracing it. Billie had done two modeling ads with the young Detroit singer and felt she was genuinely a good person.

Something you didn't often see in the music industry.

"I would like to first thank the DeLoines family for having me, and I would also like to say congratulations to Billie. She accomplished a huge feat, and your man is proud of you," Naiyana spoke staring Billie's way.

A few people clapped as Billie grinned. She nodded, and Naiyana began to sing. Billie turned her attention to Dreux and his eyes seared love into her. She swallowed hard as she sat up in her seat.

"I will forever love you Dreux. I mean forever baby. This means a lot to me, baby."

Dreux shook his head.

"Calm down beautiful. Don't thank me for shit I'm supposed to be doing. Just keep up the good work. That's what you do," he told her.

Billie nodded as she smiled so hard that her cheeks hurt.

"I will baby," she murmured hoping she was strong enough to stay on the straight and narrow path.

Malachi seemed to be adamant on making her life a living hell, and with all the stress he pushed her way it did give her the urge to drink.

After having dinner and listening to the singer croon out two songs, Billie and Dreux retreated upstairs in the snazzy hotel. Billie's eyes widened as they crossed the threshold. The presidential suite was fit for a queen and king. Rose petals covered the floor while lit candles sat on the glass table near the door and the bar top.

Facing the couple was a perfect view of the Detroit River thanks to the floor to ceiling windows. Billie quickly stepped out of her shoes as Dreux rolled up a blunt.

"You like it?" he asked sealing his cigar.

Billie walked around the large room and headed towards the bedroom.

"Stop asking silly questions baby. I freaking love this place, and you better smoke that shit outside. They might kick our black asses up out of here for doing that," she semi-joked.

Dreux chuckled. He stood up from the sofa and cleared his throat.

"Shit they might. Give me a sec," he replied as she headed into the room.

Billie entered the bedroom of the suite and soaked in the luxury of the room. A large king-sized bed sat in the center of the room and was flanked by two small nightstands. Gold and glass lamps sat on the nightstands while a large shiny black dresser faced the bed. On it was a large plasma that played soft Jazz music.

The walls in the bedroom had an incredibly unique watercolor print, and it made you feel like you were inside of a

61

castle. Everything was upscale. The best of the best and once again Dreux had outdone himself.

"This fucking man of mine," she whispered taking off her top.

Large hands stopped her from removing her clothing and the strong stench of marijuana filled the space around her. Billie closed her eyes as his soft lips brushed against her neck.

"Let's take a shower," he demanded in a way so sexy, so alluring that she immediately nodded.

Dreux led Billie into the large bathroom, and the elegant style of the hotel once again floored her. They quietly de-clothed and when they were naked, they entered the glass shower. Billie let Dreux turn on the water as she ran her hands through her long mane.

Dreux turned to her as the large shower head sprayed out the hot water and he pulled her into his arms. His hands cupped her ass as he pressed his big dick into her.

"I know what happened in the past weighs heavily on you, but I want you to promise me you will try to let it go. Kawan is okay, and so are you. He doesn't even remember the shit baby. You stopped drinking and got your shit back right. You will be okay, ma," he promised.

Dreux picked Billie up and her legs wrapped around his waist. As his member instinctively found her opening, she gazed into his eyes. They were low and red-rimmed due to his weed smoking still she saw the love. Billie knew that the moment she looked into his eyes and didn't see the love that they had a problem.

"How do you know I will be okay? Look at my mom. This addictive nature could still be on me."

Dreux shook his head. He rocked Billie at a slow pace up and down on his fat penis head.

"Why even put that shit on you? Yeah, generational curses are real, but we can pray that off you. I thought that was what we were doing ma. You talking too defeated for my liking and I don't like that shit. That's not you, and we both know that. Kiss me with your pretty ass," he demanded.

Billie leaned towards him and when her lips pressed against his, that big ass extension that Dreux knew as his dick slid into Billie. Her eyes briefly closed as he filled her up whole.

"Oh God. Baby," she moaned.

Lost in pleasure, she held on tightly to Dreux. He slapped her ass and dug deeper. His eyes never left her face as he went as far as he could go inside of her love canal.

"Damn. You feel so good. Squeeze my dick," he requested in a breathy tone.

Billie did as he asked, and he grunted out in pleasure. Dreux took Billie to the closest wall and pounded into her as he lowered his head to lick on her nipples. Her hands rubbed at his curly taper as his tongue slithered over her sensitive areolas.

Billie's heart raced and her pleasure spiked. Her spine straightened and seconds later her walls secreted for Dreux. She pulled at his hair as her body came apart for him.

Dreux groaned and fucked her harder. His teeth sunk into her fat nipple and she whimpered. Dreux had the kind of dick that drove you mad. She was positive that if he ever gave her dick away, she would make the news.

"Baby I'ma cum again," she breathed out.

Dreux chuckled. He pulled her away from the wall and took her over to the shower head. Water beat down hard on Billie's back as he raised her up and down onto his shaft.

"You saying that like it's a bad thing. Stop whining and bust all over this dick. Fuck you waiting for? Wet me up," he instructed and fucked her harder.

Billie's jaw fell open as she cried out. She allowed for her head to fall back and as the water hit her face her body orgasmed for Dreux once more.

A few days later Billie strolled alongside Normani inside of Allure boutique. Billie grabbed a few shirts that caught her eye before glancing over at her girl. Normani like always was in fashion heaven. Her buggy was filled to the brim with clothing and accessories.

Billie laughed to herself as she watched Normani fawn over a pair of ripped high waisted jeans that the designer had made. With Normani's eclectic style Billie was relieved to see that she was able to find so much clothing that suited her unique taste.

Like today while Billie wore a strapless black dress with

Fendi kicks and the matching logo waist belt that she put around her

shoulder as a crossbody, Normani wore oversized jeans with

platform heels and a hot pink baby Tommy Girl Tee. On

Normani's face was her adorable retro style Dior reading glasses.

Billie loved when Normani took out the contacts and embraced her

lenses. They looked beautiful on her.

"Like always you killing shit. How have things been going for

you?" Billie asked.

From her friendship with Novah, she met Normani.

Normani was nine years younger than Billie still they clicked.

Normani was like her baby sister, and since Billie didn't have any

siblings, she'd gladly made Normani her baby sis as well.

It was only right.

"It's been going. Tru has been out of town for a week now,

so I've been in the house with River going crazy. He won't even take

my calls," Normani replied with sad eyes.

Billie watched her pick up a pair of ripped jeans and toss

them into her already full shopping cart.

"But I see he gave you some money. You in here going dumb like this stuff cheap."

Normani smiled sadly and shook her head.

"I took it before he left. Lately mom and Novah been on me tough about money, so I've resorted to snaffling some of his cash. I refuse to have that baby and me inside of that house with no funds. You know? Leaving him seems like it's my only recourse," Normani replied.

Billie nodded hating the despair she saw covering Normani's face.

"I hate seeing you like this. I remember when you first met Tru you were so happy. So full of life and I loved that. I didn't agree when you dropped out of school, but I didn't judge. I know how I feel about Dreux, so I didn't question it. However, I don't believe in losing yourself in a man. So many women get a man and forget about the life they had before them. You can't put yourself to the side to sit up under him. That just doesn't make any sense sis. You're usually full of smiles and laughter. He's dimming your light, and now you need to ask yourself how much more are you going to allow for him to take? Don't wait until the light is out either. Trust me when I say it's much easier to bounce back when you have something left in you. Can your insanely smart behind understand that?" she asked going from serious to playful with her response.

Normani smiled revealing her pretty set of white teeth.

"I think I can then there's AZ. He's back for good," Normani said, and Billie whistled.

AZ better known as Azariah was Normani's high school sweetheart. They'd dated from ten to twelfth grade and broke up before he left for college. What drew Normani and Billie, so close together was that their backgrounds with Azariah and Dreux was similar. They had both fallen for men that was once their best friends. The only difference was Billie now had her man back while Normani was stuck between her daughters' father and her ex-boyfriend.

"Aww shit. My boy back and he coming for his girls huh?"

Normani waved off Billie while cheesing.

"He hasn't called me yet. I saw him post on IG that he was home for good and he was at his new building. He was looking good too. Like really fucking good Billie and I felt guilty. I still love Tru. I'm still in love with Tru."

Billie looked over at Normani and smiled at her.

"Then why the talk of Azariah? You know your mom once told me that a lonely heart would feed off anything. Are you fawning over your ex because of Tru once again pushing you to the side or is it because you genuinely miss him?" Billie asked.

Normani stared at a pretty collared shirt as she shrugged.

"A little of both. I never had sex with Azariah so I do shamefully fantasize about what that would be like, but it also has a lot to do with Tru. He's all over the place with me. At first, I could keep up, but his intermittent behavior is too much now. Somethings shifting with us and it scares me," Normani revealed to her.

Billie leaned towards Normani and pulled on her straight strand of silky black hair that hung to her breast.

"I think you're shifting sis. Little sis is growing up and seeing that the shit she put up with before isn't what she wants to put up with now. Embrace it," Billie told her as her friend and boutique owner Mickey walked over.

"Looking good Billie! That's why I need you for my new shoot and who is this girl over here looking like my twin," Mickey said walking up.

Billie laughed and exchanged quick hugs with Mickey before looking at Normani. It was then that she saw Normani and Mickey did favor one another. They were both chocolate toned women with high cheekbones and wide, bright smiles. However, when it came to the bodies, they differed. Normani was slim thick while Mickey was plain old thick. The kind of thickness that only food or genes could give you.

"This is my best friends' sister Normani who is also like my little sister," Billie replied.

Normani smiled as she looked at Mickey.

"It's so nice to meet you! I see you online all the time, and your baby daddy is fine as hell..." Normani stopped talking and covered her mouth. Mickey laughed as Normani shook her head. "I didn't mean that disrespectfully, I just saw him on your page a few times. He knows my man," she explained.

Mickey waved her off, and Billie admired how cute Mickey was looking in her simple get-up of jeans and a white linen top. Mickey's hair was in a natural puffball as curls billowed out the top of her band. Her skin held a glow to it as she looked at Billie and Normani.

"Easton knows everybody with his mean ass. I love your outfit and glasses. Who styles you?" Mickey asked Normani.

Normani shook her head.

"Me," she replied making Mickey and Billie laughed lightly.

"I love it. You're so fine it's insane, just like our Billie over here. I would love for you two, to do a few ads for me. Would you all be down?" Mickey asked looking between Billie and Normani.

Normani shook her head while Billie smiled widely.

"I'd love too," Billie told her friend.

"I can't but thanks for the offer," Normani said quietly.

Mickey nodded.

"It's cool and Billie I'll hit you up in a few days with the details. I have to go pick up my son so I will see you all later," Mickey said before walking away.

Billie watched her friend walk off before glancing over at Normani.

"That could have been a check for you. Why did you turn it down?"

Normani sighed. She cleared her throat as she looked Billie's way.

71

"The camera is for you, but I'm cool on all that plus I wouldn't want my big ass glasses and colorful clothes on display like that. Let's check out so we can go," she replied and walked off.

Billie shook her head as she watched Normani walk up to the counter with her cart full of clothing. For Normani to be as smart as she was, she sometimes lacked common sense. She was gorgeous with a bomb ass unique style. Billie hated that she didn't see that about herself.

After spending $2000 at Allure Boutique, Billie took Normani home and headed to Malachi's house. Her anxiousness to see her son set her nerves on fire as she pulled into Malachi's driveway. Actually, his mother's driveway since he didn't want to move from his mothers' home.

Billie shut off her car and called Malachi. One of the rules he set in place for her to see Kawan was that she had to let him know the minute she pulled up. Billie thought it was silly but to stay on his good side, she was willing to do whatever she had to.

"You here?" Malachi's deep agitated voice asked as he took the call.

Billie rolled her eyes as she stared out of the window at the two-story brick home.

"Yes, I told you I would call when I was outside. Is he up?"

"Aye! Don't call with all that fucking attitude. You need to get through me to see him. I'm not at home right now, but my mom is. Just ring the doorbell and send me a pic of you two together. Since he stays with me, he be wanting to see your face sometimes and shit," Malachi griped before ending the call.

Billie's brows bunched together as she grabbed her bag and exited her car.

"Old dumb ass nigga," she muttered hiking up the walkway.

Before Billie could walk up the steps, the front door opened, and her son Kawan rushed out of the home smiling. Billie met him halfway and picked him up. Kawan laughed heartily, and she playfully tossed him into the air.

"That boy know he loves his momma," Malachi's mother Cindy said stepping onto the porch.

Billie nodded as she kissed her son all over his mocha shaded face.

"And I love him too. How you doing Ms. Cindy?"

Cindy smiled while smoothing out her jet-black shoulder-length hair.

"Good and you know to call me momma, girl."

Billie nodded choosing not to respond. Cindy liked to play both sides of the fence and because of that Billie handled her ass with a long-handled spoon.

"Come in, come in. Let's catch up," Cindy insisted before going back into the house.

Billie sat her son down and grabbed his bags from her trunk before walking with him into the home. Like always the two-story house reeked of cigarettes and cheap perfume. Billie's nose wrinkled in disgust as she led her son to the living room.

This bitch smoke so much she gone give my son lung problems.

"Now what's been up Billie? You didn't come to my party last month," Cindy said pulling out a small bottle of wine.

She sipped from the bottle and Billie stared at the drink briefly before handing her son the toys from the bags. One of the things Billie agreed to do was provide weekly for Kawan. It wasn't court ordered, but it was a request from Malachi. Billie bought

74

Kawan's clothing and whatever else he needed and did it happily.

She felt that Malachi should be buying him things as well, but

because her son was living with him, she didn't put up a fight.

Billie's only goal was to get her child back.

"I was sick, and Malachi didn't want me to come," she

replied truthfully.

Cindy frowned as she finished off her wine. Billie pocketed

the receipt from the items she'd bought, and Kawan sat in the

middle of the family room in toy land.

"He's such a loser girl. Don't act like shit but his sorry ass,

lying ass, cheating ass daddy. All he does is hang out with his boys

and beg his cousins to hang with him. You know they see him as a

child, baby. Hell, he's the only one of them that's not doing

anything worth speaking about with his life. Well him and Donny.

He makes a little change at his factory job, but it's nothing compared

to Deidra's youngest boy. I keep telling him to do something with

himself, so I can rub it in my sister's face. I can't stand her," Cindy

said and laughed to herself.

Billie offered her a tight-lipped smile and stared back down

at her son. She noticed his unkept fade, dirty attire and frowned. On top of buying Kawan clothing and toys, she also sent Malachi money

weekly. Money that really came from her man so she couldn't

understand why her son was looking like one of the fucking lost

boys at the moment.

"Ms. Cindy when was the last time he took him to get his

hair cut?"

Cindy sat back in her recliner and sighed. She passed gas

before grabbing the cable remote.

"Chile don't get me to lying. I told you, Malachi—"

"Malachi what?"

His voice always made her stomach knot up. She wasn't

afraid of him, but she was worried about the things he could do to

her when it came to Kawan. Billie glanced back at her ex-friend

because he'd never been her man and she sighed. He was the one

man that followed her around like a lost puppy for years.

The one man that was her shoulder to cry on. One sad

drunken night while she'd retreated to Malachi's home to complain

about Dreux and how much she missed him sex happened. Billie

was still fuzzy as to how because she couldn't even remember the

act, but it did occur. Kawan was proof of that, and it had only been once. Billie never slept with Malachi again but let him tell it they had

a loving relationship. She was convinced that he was partially crazy.

He had to because of the lies he constantly made up about her.

"About why you haven't gotten his hair cut," Billie replied

still staring up at him.

She made sure to speak it nicely however the frown marring

Malachi's chunky face told her he was pissed. She watched him walk

his 5'9 frame into the family room, and Billie assessed his looks.

Whereas Kawan wore old dirty threads, Malachi was fresh as fuck

from head to toe. Robin Jeans shorts with a white crew neck and

new Jordan's was his get up. He also sported a crisp taper along with

a sparkly chain. Billie swallowed hard as she stared at him.

"Your haircut is nice," she noted quietly.

Cindy snickered until Malachi glared over at her. He'd

picked up weight Billie realized, and she guessed that he was close

to 250 pounds maybe more. The look wasn't becoming of him.

"I'm taking him in the morning. I been working all damn

week. I had to do that so he could eat. While you been doing what?

Sitting on ya ass," he snapped.

Cindy slowly stood and quietly exited the living room.

Billie's eyes ventured down to her son, and she watched him play with his new toys. Her leg bounced as she stared back up at Malachi.

"I can get him during the week Malachi. That's not an issue for me."

Malachi quickly shook his head.

"Hell no! And nearly kill him again? You must be fucking crazy. I know you on this brand-new Billie shit, but I see through it, ma. You still a lush," he quipped before chuckling.

Billie stood and went over to her son. She kissed his forehead and whispered words of love into his ear. As she looked over at Malachi, she frowned.

"The judge will see what I've done, and I will be granted days with him. Visitations that I won't have to go through you to handle because the judge will set it. I'm showing you that I changed. It's not right for you to behave this way towards me and please watch your language around him," Billie said calmly.

Malachi's jaw twitched as he took a step towards Billie.

"Watch my language? After what you did, me cussing not gone fucking hurt him. The judge might grant you visitation, but that's where it's gone stop. I'm still working and supporting him. They won't take him away from me," Malachi said arrogantly.

Billie nodded. Her eyes took in the cluttered family room, and a deep ache filled her belly. She wanted her son with her now. Malachi and his mother were toxic. They meant her child no good and could only show him negative things to do. Hell, they would only show him what they knew which wasn't much.

"We'll have to see about that Malachi," she replied.

"Take your wanna be a momma ass on, man. New acting ass. You ain't changed. You still a partying ass broad that only thinks of herself. Too selfish to even be with me so that we can be a family. You ain't shit," Malachi grumbled with angry eyes.

As she walked away, Malachi chuckled darkly. Billie quickened her steps so that he wouldn't see her cry. She'd already shed so many tears but what she refused to do was allow for Malachi to pull any more of them up out of her.

The next day Billie sat inside of Allure Boutique talking with her good friend Mickey. She hadn't expected to be back so soon but was planning on meeting up with Reese and figured the boutique was a nice place to do it. As she waited on Reese to show up, she caught up with her girl. Billie and Mickey had many things in common along with the fact that they both didn't have custody of their kids.

"How is your son doing? I miss his handsome little butt," Billie noted.

Mickey smiled as she wiped down her glass jewelry case.

"He's good. Easton has him out of town visiting people that were related to his foster mom. They should be back in town later today. How is Kawan?"

Billie thought of her son and sighed. Her talk with Malachi hung heavy on her heart as she replayed his hateful words. He was merely a shitty ass person because it seemed he only wanted her to be doing bad.

"He's good. I'm counting down the time for me to get some days with him. I go to court in a month, and I'm ready. Malachi isn't shit Mickey. I send over money, I buy clothes, and his fat ass can't even take my baby to get his damn haircut. I'm so tired of dealing with him. You have it so good with Easton. He practically lets EJ live with you although he has full custody of him," Billie replied.

Mickey nodded. She sat her cleaning items down and peered at Billie intently. She cleared her throat as she stared Billie's way.

"I am lucky in terms of that but don't get it confused. I want my son back as well. It's just things are delicate between Easton and myself. I feel guilty much like you do. Just the thought of taking him to court makes my head spin. I'm not prepared either to bring up such sad emotions. When I was lost to the world, those were the worst days of my life. I'm happy now, but life could be better." Mickey stopped talking and smiled sweetly at Billie. "Like much fucking better but for the moment I'm content."

Billie nodded understanding completely where Mickey was coming from.

"You still love him Mickaela?" she asked calling Mickey out by her government.

Mickey blushed as she looked away from Billie.

"With every breath in my body Billie," she said in a tone laced with yearning and pain.

81

Billie pulled her friend into a hug as Reese walked up.

"I love this boutique. I always wanted to come here," Reese gushed as Mickey pulled away from Billie.

Mickey discreetly wiped her eyes and shot Reese a warm smile.

"Hi and excuse me, ladies," Mickey said before walking off.

Billie looked Reese over and smiled. Like before Reese looked beautiful with a youthful glow that only a young age could give you.

"How old are you?"

"Nineteen but I feel like I'm fifty," Reese replied.

Billie nodded knowing the feeling. When life was hard, it had a way of making you feel much older than what you were. Billie cleared her throat as she looked over the beautiful young woman.

"How did you start drinking?"

Reese licked her lips. She fidgeted with the hem of her shirt as she stared up at Billie.

"I fell into the college life. Party after party and before I knew it, I was hooked. I was drinking to get through the day. I loved the escape that it brought me. College was hard for me. I'm in no way putting this on my family, but they rode me hard as well. Hell, they still do, and, in their eyes, I am expected to be perfect. I'm the girl that can do no wrong when no one can live up to that standard. I'm not Jesus, I sin, but they seem to think otherwise," she responded.

Billie thought back on her wild years, and she empathized with Reese. Their stories were similar in ways.

"Well, I started drinking when I was fifteen. I have been modeling since I was a baby. My mom always said that my baby pictures from the hospital was so nice that everyone wanted a copy. It was like I was born to do it. Once I became a teenager, I realized that a lot of the people I modeled with were getting high and always drinking. Honestly, I fell victim to it out of peer pressure and young age. I was left alone because they trusted me to work, but I was also a kid. I needed them there and because my family wasn't it left me to make adult decisions that my immature mind wasn't capable of making. My story ended badly, however. I crashed my car with my son in and ended up losing custody of him. When I woke up in that hospital, I knew that liquor wasn't for me. I knew that it was my downfall and at that moment I chose to walk away. Do you need a

wakeup call like mine to let it go?" Billie asked.

Reese's eyes narrowed as she shook her head.

"I've already let it go."

Billie smiled. She grabbed a top that she knew would look

cute with her fitted jeans and she glanced over at Reese.

"You've been drinking today, but you let it go? I can smell it

on you, but it's fine. Like you said we are all sinners. The thing is

you can't acknowledge you have a problem then keep doing it. I'm

going to sponsor you Reese but only if you want to change."

Reese's shoulders sagged as she looked away from Billie.

"I am. I needed a drink earlier to deal with my family, but I

swear I'm done now. You can even test me."

Billie rubbed her arm to soothe her mind.

"I'm not your P.O. I simply want to be your friend and

listening ear. I'm always available to talk and hang out. I want to

help you in any way that I can," Billie said sincerely, and Reese

looked back to her.

Reese's eyes glazed over as she slowly nodded.

"You're the first person that's told me that, and I believe them."

Billie smiled as she envisioned seeing Reese free from her alcohol abuse. Billie knew it was possible because she herself was a walking testimony to what prayer, and dedication could do for you.

"And I mean it. God blessed me, and I have to pay it forward. I believe it's why he kept me alive. To be better than I was before. To serve out his purpose and part of that is saving people that like me have an addiction to alcohol," Billie replied, and Reese nodded before they finished up their meeting.

Two days later Dreux stepped into his mothers' clean home. Soft gospel music played throughout the living room as he stepped out of his $1000 sneakers. His eyes peered around the swanky, and he searched for the woman he loved so much.

A heavy breath escaped him as he walked further into the home.

"Ma, where you at!"

"In the dining room and stop with all that yelling Dreux," Deidra fussed.

Dreux chuckled as he headed towards his mother. He found her seconds later sitting at her cherry oak dining table with a stack of bills before her. His smile fell as he joined her at the table. Dreux inspected his mother's pristine looks for a minute. Deidra was a curvaceous woman with a big smile and slanted light brown eyes. She usually wore her hair in soft curls that reached the top of her shoulder while rocking the latest threads. Dreux had never known his father. Didn't even ask about the nigga and to him, his mom was both parents. Always had been. Deidra worked hard as an engineer to give her sons a good life. Dreux watched his mother suffer from his brother becoming a drug dealer, and he vowed to never put her through that. Instead, he'd chosen college and was trying his best to make her the proudest mother she could be. She deserved the world, and he worked hard to give it to her. Because of Dreux, she lived in a beautiful two-story brownstone in Canton. She also had a foreign car due to her sons giving ways.

Dreux always had to force his mother to take his gifts because she hated the thought of him spending so much cash, but after much convincing, he was able to get her to take them.

"What's good with you, young lady?" he asked cheesing at her.

Deidra smiled. She looked up from her bills and sat back in her seat. The small diamonds in her ears sparkled as she stared at her youngest son.

"I'm good. I talked to your brother earlier. It's looking like he may be home in the next two months."

Dreux nodded. His brother had been approved for early release due to him attending a few classes while locked up. He'd been gone for years, and Dreux was excited as shit to see him.

"Yeah, he told me. I'm ready I just don't wanna get excited, and they change it at the last minute. You know how they do."

Deidra nodded. Dreux grabbed the bill that sat in front of his mother and his eyes scanned the paper. His mother's calm resolve turned to worry as he looked back up at her.

"What's this?"

Deidra shook her head. She tried to grab the bill, and he held onto it tighter.

"How is work coming along?" she asked changing the subject.

Dreux read over the bill again and his insides boiled with anger.

"Ma why the fuck does it say you owe your bank $40,000. What's going on?"

"What you're not about to do is sit up in here and curse at me. Respect the woman that brought you into this world," she replied with a tight mouth.

Dreux nodded immediately regretting his choice of words.

"And I do. I'm sorry now what's this about? You not broke ma, we far from that. What's going on?"

Deidra fiddled with her gold Tiffany's ring that Dreux had given her two Christmas's ago.

"Your auntie called me. She said she was losing her house and she needed for me to co-sign on a loan with her. As much as that woman works my nerves, I didn't want to see her or them babies out on the street, so I did—"

Dreux's face tightened at his mother's response. He chuckled to keep his cool.

"Them babies? You must be speaking on Kawan cause Malachi's hefty's as-.... he ain't no baby ma."

Deidra nodded.

"I know that, but she needed it Dreux. Her home was in foreclosure, and she had one last chance to save it. I signed on with her, and she was making payments, but she recently stopped so now they're coming after me. Every time I go to her house, she refuses to come to the door. She done even stopped coming to church all because she doesn't want to see me. I decided to stop calling because I refuse to chase anybody," his mother replied.

Dreux's leg bounced as his mind drifted to a dark place. He could handle people trying to fuck him over any day of the week but his mom? She was off limits. Like a precious jewel, she was never to be touched. Never to be played with yet their own family was the guilty party. For as long as Dreux could remember his auntie had been jealous of his mom. Much like her son Malachi was jealous of him. While Malachi had a love, hate game he played with Dreux his mother had a straight up hatred towards Deidra. Dreux couldn't understand why his mom would even take her phone call let alone sign on a loan with her. Shit didn't make any sense to him.

Dreux sat the paper down and cleared his throat. The protectiveness he felt over his mom had him heated, but with her, he needed to remain calm. He took a deep breath and exhaled. His hand brushed over his curls on his head as he looked his mother's way. She was too nice, and the thing about being nice was people usually fucked you over, but this was one loss Dreux refused to let his mom take.

Nah, his auntie was going to have to rectify the shit she'd done to his mother.

"Ma, why would you co-sign for her? I don't get it. She don't even like you."

Deidra smiled at her sons' words. She neatly stacked the papers before her and looked up at her child.

"My love for my family isn't conditional. There are things that happened between me and my sister that has shaped us into the sisters that we now are. I won't take all the blame, but I can say that I haven't always been a good sister to her son. I do get why she's upset, so I let a lot of the things that she does slide. I still love her son and I always will. I'm still waiting on the day for her to be the sister that I grew up with. Until then I will be waiting. I couldn't watch her get kicked out like that," she replied.

Dreux rubbed at his temples. His anger was mounting, and his mother wasn't making it any better. She was a God-fearing woman no doubt, but she was taking her Christianity to another level.

"I got you. I'ma pay it off today," he said and put the bill into his back pocket.

Deidra opened her mouth to protest, and Dreux shot her a look that made her simply nod.

"It wasn't my intention to have you do that son. I was going to take some money from my savings and pay half now and the rest in a few months. I can do it," she told him.

Dreux's eyes looked his mother over, and he smirked at her.

"As long as I'm alive you won't have to. Business is good, and I'm thankful for that. You ready for your trip?"

Deidra's face lit up, and she smiled. Dreux was sending her and her church sisters on a trip to Mexico for the weekend.

"Of course I am. How is my Billie doing?"

The mention of Billie's name made Dreux relax. Just the thought of her put him in a better mood. He could only think of one time he'd ever hated hearing her name, and it was after

everything had come out with, she and Malachi.

"She good. I been thinking bout telling Malachi about us.

This hiding not for me. I mean I don't feel guilty anyway cause she

was never his girl, but since they got Kawan, I do feel kind of bad.

Still, he knew from the jump how I felt about her. It wasn't a secret

and for him to play that move showed me that he's not real. She

even showed me back then all the stuff he'd showed her just to

make her feel like I was with Kylie. You know I never cared for

Kylie like I do Billie and he knew that too. Honestly, I'm only

keeping quiet because she asked me to. You know I would have

been let him know. I might even go behind her back and tell him,"

he replied.

Deidra cleared her throat as her eyes widened.

"I'm not sure about that son. I think you need to give this

more time. I know you don't want to hide it forever, but it's a

delicate situation. I would wait some more. How do you think Billie

would feel if you snuck and told him?" she asked.

Dreux shook his head. He ran his hand over his soft hair

and sighed.

"She probably wouldn't like it, but I'm a man at the end of the day. This sneaking around not for me. We been hiding this for two years. I'm ready to marry that girl. Give her a ring and a new crib, but I'm not doing any of that until he knows. It's only right."

His mother nodded as she stared at him.

"Yes, I agree, but please wait a little longer. I don't see this ending well Dreux. Give Billie some more time," his mom pleaded.

Dreux nodded with a frown marring his face. All that waiting shit was for the birds. He wanted Billie to be his wife but for that to happen, Malachi, had to know about them. He wasn't popping the question until everyone knew of their relationship especially his bitch ass cousin.

3

#ssdd

Her straight strands stretched to an unbelievable rate as he tugged them as hard as he could. Her doe-shaped eyes the same shade as maple syrup lolled to the back of her head as he drove his member into her repeatedly.

Normani tried to push back and fight off the intrusion from his thickness, and he slapped her hand away.

"Nah, you wanna flip out every second of the damn day. I know what you need, ma. Calm down and take this dick," Tru demanded.

Normani's thighs began to shake, and Tru chuckled.

"There she go," he muttered before leaning down. His thick lips planted wet kisses across Normani's neck as he pumped into

94

her as hard as he could. "Close your eyes and let go. Let my pussy cum," he demanded sexily in her ear.

Normani's heart rate spiked as tears pricked her eyes. She clawed at the sheets as she felt her orgasm overtake her.

"Tru...Tru slow down," she begged helplessly.

Tru licked his lips. He shoved his long tongue into Normani's ear as his dick knocked at her g-spot. Within seconds Normani's body exploded for him. Her legs gave out, and she collapsed onto the California king-sized mattress. Tru went down with her pumping away as he chased his own release.

"Damn, that pussy still cumming?" he asked in a throaty tone.

Normani offered a faint yes as her vagina pulsated for him. Her walls tightened, and Tru growled into her neck as his back stiffened. For several minutes he rested on top of Normani as they both tried to catch their breath.

"Waaaa! Waaaa! Ma-ma! Waaa!"

The loud cries of their daughter made Tru pull back. Slowly he removed himself from Normani's sex before falling out onto the bed. Normani sat up slowly with her chest heaving up and down.

She ran her hands through her frizzy sweated out strands and sighed.

"We need a nanny."

Tru chuckled.

"You keep taking it like that, and we'll get two of them bitches," he joked.

Normani glanced back at him and licked her pouty lips.

"I'm serious. I work assiduously with River, but it can be tiring at times. We can afford it Tru so why not?"

Tru nodded. His downcast eyes gazed up at Normani as he pulled the comforter up over his toned, tatted up naked body.

"What's up with this we shit? Don't you mean me? I can barely afford to take care of y'all with as much as you spend. How the fuck I go to sleep with ten g's on me and wake up broke? Fuck kind of shit is that Normani and what I say about talking like that? Use regular fucking words baby. A nigga was barely able to graduate high school in this bitch."

Normani found her strength to stand and she smiled. She snatched her silk Sailor Moon kimono robe from the floor and quickly put it on.

"But you did graduate and look at you now. You're the best DJ to ever do it Tru. If you were to put me on your actual account, not the dummy one you wouldn't have to worry about waking up broke. Until then I'ma continue to hit your pockets, honey," she replied.

Normani went to grab her glasses and Tru sucked his teeth.

"Come on ma. It's too early to be walking round this bitch in them large ass frames. Where your contacts at?" he asked.

Normani sighed. She looked at Tru and his eyes connected with her's.

"Tru I get tired of putting them things in. The glasses are easy to wear."

Tru nodded. He licked his lips as he gazed her way.

"You beautiful as hell ma, but I love to see your whole face. Them shits cover half of it. Do it for me," he begged lowly.

Normani rolled her eyes as she sat her prescription glasses down. She went into the bathroom and quickly put in her contacts before exiting her bedroom.

Normani found her fourteen-month-old daughter standing in her crib when she entered her room. Beside her was her princess pull-up resting on the mattress. Normani shook her head as she picked her chunky fair skinned baby up.

"I guess you were in here crying us a river huh?"

River smiled with crocodile tears falling down her fat cheeks. Normani smiled at her daughter and sat her on the floor. River rushed over to her corner of toys as Normani grabbed fresh underwear and a onesie. Normani quietly dressed her daughter before leaving out of the bedroom. Normani took her daughter downstairs to the kitchen and placed her in the high chair.

Like they did every morning Normani began breakfast while her daughter watched her educational videos. Once Normani was done cooking she pulled out her flashcards and held them up for River to see.

"Point to the color pink," Normani told her holding up a pink and a blue card.

River smiled and quickly pointed to pink.

"Ink!" River said attempting to say the word.

Normani smiled like a proud momma and held up another set of cards.

"Okay point to the car baby," she instructed.

River looked back and forth between the cards before pointing to the red car.

"Ar!" she yelled.

"Damn she smart as shit. Its kids bigger than her and they can't talk yet," Tru said coming into the kitchen.

Bond. 9 floated around Normani's space making her frown. He only wore that cologne when he was preparing to be gone for a few days.

Normani sat the cards down and looked back at her man. From the moment she'd met Tru in the club she'd been smitten with him. Yes, she was attractive, that was something she never questioned, but men like Tru didn't regularly come on to her. To Normani he was the cream of the crop. The sexiest nigga she'd ever seen alive, and while he was rough around the edges even rocking facial tattoo's, he was handsome. Handsome in the kind of way that made you cream yourself. He was a cutie. Tall standing at 6'4 with a lean build and handsome face. He usually wore up to date designer threads and was always sporting the flyest shoes. He had a thing for nice ass kicks. Tru rocked his hair in low cut waves with a neatly groomed beard. His skin was the color of coffee with way too much milk in it and Normani was positive River had gotten her complexion and fine silky black hair from her daddy.

Tru couldn't deny his daughter even if he wanted to.

"You just got home. Where you off to now?"

Tru frowned at Normani's question. He placed his diamond chain around his neck and made a silly face at River before turning his attention back to Normani.

"Out. I need to meet with some people and holla at this nigga Kasam. You know he be having them hookups for me and shit. I'm trying to tour with them niggas he used to manage. I'll be back by eight so find a sitter. Preferably my momma or yours," he replied.

Tru laced Normani with a kiss to her forehead before walking away.

Normani looked back to her daughter as Tru exited the house and River smiled at her. Normani shook her head as she pulled another set of cards out.

"Your chunky butt looks just like your daddy," she told her, and River laughed like she knew what she was saying.

Hours skated by like minutes as Normani anticipated her date with Tru. She took River to her mothers' home and got her hair curled into sexy spiral curls just the way Tru liked before returning home.

That was at 8 pm.

At 9 pm she was showered and dressed in a black Versace dress that hugged her body tightly. One of Tru's favorite dresses. He often told her that he liked the way it made her curves pop out. Normani was on the smaller side, but she packed a mean punch in her little frame.

At 11 pm Normani sat inside of her living room with a glass of wine. Her eyes stared down at her freshly painted toes. The white polish again one of Tru's favorites looked perfect against her chocolate skin. Her watery lenses glanced up at her glass chandelier that cost more money than the shit was worth, and she sighed.

"He's such a mendacious ass nigga."

The words escaped her lips quietly.

Angrily even because once again he's stood her up.

He came home, fucked her so good it made her cry then lied to her.

At one in the morning, Normani found herself drunk as hell. Tru was officially ignoring her calls and all the fucks she had to give about him for the day was done with. Normani rose from the seat slowly and rubbed her bottom. Her ass was asleep. She'd been sitting in the chair for so long even her legs were numb.

"Why do I keep dealing with this? I mean why? I have to be a dense ass broad to allow for him to keep playing me," she muttered.

Normani walked sluggishly through her home. Slowly she ascended the steps and went into her bedroom. Her eyes traveled around the room deliberately. While anger coursed through her like lava. She wanted to kill him. Kill his black ass dead then love him back to life. That was the sort of insane shit he evoked out of her, and she knew it wasn't right. Couldn't have been normal and even if it was, she refused for it to be her normal any longer.

"I'm trying you know. I'm trying to give my baby what I had, but he's making it damn near impossible," she mumbled heading for the bathroom.

Normani kicked off her heels in the process, and as she reached the bathroom, her eyes ventured over to Tru's closet.

Normani made a quick detour and went into his haven. Her eyes roamed around the large space as her heart pumped fast. She stared at his clothes, shoes, and jewelry before glancing back at his sneakers. They had to be worth at least half a million dollars.

A quick thought flashed through her mind, and she shook it off.

"Nah, I can't Left Eye my own house," she mumbled.

Normani exited the closet and grabbed her house phone. She sat at the edge of her bed and called the one person that she knew would put her mind at ease. The one person that she hadn't spoken to in months because Tru always pitched a fit whenever they spoke. However tonight it was fuck him and how he felt. Shit, he was showing her that she wasn't number one to him and she was ready to show him the same.

"Damn you calling a nigga from the landline and shit. You like the only person I know with a damn house phone. You good? Or wait is this my nigga Tru?" Azariah asked and chuckled.

Normani smiled to herself as her tears slipped from her eyes. She hated that her first time speaking back to him had to be in such a way.

"Whatever," she breathed into the phone quietly. "Your home for good yet you didn't call me?"

Azariah sighed. The music in his background was lowered as he breathed into the phone.

"Look Tru be on that shit that I can't fuck with. Nigga calling my phone with dry ass threats and shit, so I had to fall back. You know me Normani. I don't do no talking. I think cause I actually gave a fuck about my life and went to college that the nigga thinks I'm soft. You need to tell your guy bout me though. I know niggas that will air his ass out, and I'm one of them. I choose to be more than what the media says I am. It ain't my fault his dumb ass can't do shit but play some fucking music off a laptop," Azariah replied.

Normani held in her laugh as she shook her head. She knew that Azariah was and would always be in his feelings about her being with Tru. She didn't regret it because Tru was her man and the father of her daughter, but she did also miss Azariah.

She actually missed the shit out of him.

"Calm down killa. Tru knows who your people is and how your family gets down. He is just worried about me and my feelings for you."

Azariah cleared his throat.

"What fucking feelings would that be? You been his woman since the nigga holla'd at you. Been said fuck me," he griped.

Normani sighed. She closed her eyes as her mind raced with thoughts of Azariah.

"I will always love you, and you know that," she admitted quietly.

Azariah sucked his teeth.

"Let's not even go there. What's up? You coming to see my new spot tomorrow?" he asked changing the subject.

Normani sighed. She too wanted to switch gears in the conversation.

"Of course, I am. Me and River we'll be there with bells on," she joked.

Azariah chuckled.

"I see your jokes still corny as hell. Why you up this late anyway? We all know your boring ass go to bed at eight."

Normani smiled. He knew her so well.

"Tru stood me up. He said that we were going out and he never came back home," she admitted quietly.

For several minutes they sat on the phone in silence until Azariah cleared his throat.

"I never met anybody as beautiful and smart as you. You know how you like to read all them stories and shit? Books about love and the nigga acting up?" he asked.

Normani licked her lips as her mind grew fuzzy. Her sleepiness was kicking in.

"Yeah," she said quietly.

"Imagine your life being like a book. Let's say right now you in a bad chapter so what you gotta do is end it — closeout that chapter and go to a new one. I don't gotta spell this shit out for you ma. If the nigga not making you happy then find one that will and I'ma tell you like this. You won't have to look far. He could be right in front of you and shit, and you didn't even know it. I'ma send over my address, and I wanna see your beautiful ass bright and fucking early. Have a goodnight sexy," he replied before ending the call.

"You too," she murmured although he'd already hung up.

Normani sat her phone down and rolled onto her side. Her eyes peered at her doorway, and she blinked when she spotted Tru standing in it. He walked in slowly looking as drunk as she felt.

106

"Didn't I say not to call that nigga no more?" he asked slowly.

Normani closed her eyes and licked her lips.

"What I remember most about my daddy was how good of a man he was. He loved my momma the right way. The kind of way that women dream about you know? I'm sure they had quarrels, but we never saw it. He was good to her and to us. I want that for River. I want her to have the life that I did and better. I can't do it by myself though, and you're showing me that you don't want that. Now I have to ask myself when will I accept it?"

The bed dipped, and Tru's large hand roamed over her small behind. The marijuana and liquor seeped from his pores as he leaned down and kissed her arm.

"Baby I'm sorry. I started drinking and lost track of time. The good thing is I was just picked up to tour with them Luca Gang niggas, so you know that's a big payday for us. I know life is hectic for me right now, but I will do better. Don't give up on me," he pleaded quietly.

Normani felt him take off her shoes before tugging down her underwear. Tru went to unzip her dress, and she shook her head.

"Don't. You don't get to stand me up again, then get some pussy. Pussy like mine is reserved for the nigga that comes home on time. Take your perfidious ass on somewhere."

Tru chuckled while tugging at the dress zipper once more and Normani abruptly sat up. She shoved him as hard as she could while glaring at him.

"Aye! Calm down. I said I lost track of time and I did. What I say about saying big ass words like that? Stop doing that shit. Got a nigga not knowing what the fuck you saying in this bitch. I ain't got time to be pulling up the dictionary. Now come here, ma. Let me make it up to you," he told her.

Normani's chest heaved up and down as she glared at Tru. Who was this man? Or had he been the same all along and she was just now seeing him for the piece of shit that he truly was?

"You must really take me for some kind of imbecile. I mean with the way I've submitted to you, I wouldn't even hold it against you at this point. You keep hurting me, and you want me to take it..." Normani shook her head as her words made her more emotional. "For years I did take it because I loved you. Because I felt so honored to just be with you, but I'm over it now. And I want

108

you to really listen to me Tru when I say that I am done taking it.

Act up again, and I'm done. I'm not fighting you. I'm not ruining

your clothes or even messing up your cars. I'm just leaving, and I'm

not turning back," she warned him while staring into his eyes.

Tru glared at Normani for a few seconds as she stared his

way. His frustration with her words showed on his handsome mug.

"I said I was sorry. Either take the apology or not but don't

start with that done talking shit. You not leaving and neither is River.

Take your ass to sleep before you piss me the fuck off in this bitch,"

he griped before falling back on the bed.

Normani laughed to keep from crying. More and more he

was disappointing her. Here she was crying out for him to love her

right, do right by her and he still wasn't hearing her.

Her shoulders sagged as she realized that breaking up her

family was a real possibility.

"I'ma piss you off huh? Well, Tru I've been pissed the fuck

off. I'm tired of your disrespectful ways. If you think I'm playing, try

me."

Silence followed her words and seconds later Tru's soft

snore flowed through the bedroom. Normani's heart ached at his actions. He was insistent on taking shit after shit on her. Instead of grabbing the pricey lamp and busting his fucking head open with it she instead stood up. With her head high and her heartbreaking, she exited the bedroom.

Tru was the kind of man that only reacted to actions. Her words did nothing for him, but she was cool with that. He could play big nigga all he wanted and allow for his foolishness to push her away. Normani loved him so very much, but like a dog, she could only take being knocked down so many times before she reacted.

This time it wouldn't be with petty things. She would leave and, on her father's, precious name she vowed to herself that she wouldn't dare go back.

"We just received your transcripts from your old school, and we are incredibly pleased to have you. A software engineering degree is right around the corner for you Ms. Royale. Of course, you know that you can always transfer to a university before you graduate. I'm not supposed to encourage it, but it is a good look to have a bigger name on your degree," the admissions counselor informed her.

Normani nodded. She held onto her sleeping daughter tightly as she stared at the brown skinned woman.

"Yes, I know. I've already given up the money for the first semester," Normani told her.

The counselor smiled.

"Yes, we received that as well. Your schedule has been emailed over to you, and if you feel bogged down with anything, there is counselors on staff that can help. Just let us know. Welcome to Oakland Community College," she said smiling brightly.

Pride coursed through Normani as she nodded. The last few days had been hard on her but what she did do was make a plan for herself. A plan for her own life because placing all of her eggs into Tru's basket just didn't make sense any longer.

"I'm pleased to be here," Normani revealed before they both stood up.

Normani took her paperwork from the counselor and exited the school. After leaving out of the community college, Normani decided to stop by Azariah's upscale condo that was located in Novi.

He'd been calling her nonstop to see why she hadn't come by, but

with Tru on her back, she hadn't been able to get away. Tru was

now back at work doing two shows out of town, and she was

relieved. Normani wanted some alone time with her friend so they

could catch up.

Anxiously she pulled through the large steel gates after

putting his code in and parked next to his matte black Land Rover.

Tru called her phone as she took her seatbelt off.

Normani wanted to send his call to voicemail, but the love

she still had for him wouldn't allow for her to do that. She answered

the call while rolling her eyes.

"What?"

Tru breathed into the phone as loud music played in the

background.

"It's nice to speak to you too. I'll be back home in a few

days. I thought we could hit up Cali for the weekend. I know how

much you love to shop out there. Maybe get that bag you wanted

from Louis. That $20,000 piece," he replied.

Normani sat back in her seat. She watched Azariah open his door and stare at her as she talked on the phone.

"We'll see," she murmured.

Before she would have been excited at the thought of going out of town. With Tru being so fickle she now told herself to relax. If they went to Cali, they did if they didn't then that was cool as well.

"What River doing?" he asked.

Normani rolled her eyes once more.

"Sleeping."

Tru sighed.

"You still mad? It's been a few days, and I said I was sorry baby. I stayed home the rest of the time I was in town. What else you want me to do?" he asked.

Normani watched Azariah step outside in his black two-piece suit with his black shirt that was unbuttoned at the collar and her tongue grew heavy. Her attention went back to the phone call she was on, and she groaned. What she didn't want to do was tell her man how to treat her. Things like that should have come natural for him.

113

"I'm fine. Do what you been doing Tru. I'm meeting up with Azariah. I'll call you back."

Normani knew it was petty, but a small part of her loved to throw Azariah in Tru's face. Daily she dealt with Tru's groupies stalking him on social media. It felt good to let him know that she could have people chasing after her the same way.

Tru chuckled.

"Oh, I get it. You flexing on me cause you bout to see that nigga? I thought we discussed you hanging with him? I don't want his bitch ass around my daughter either," Tru complained.

At least someone is.

"We're friends, and you know that. He's back home, and I wanted to hang out with him. Nothing more."

"Fuck that nothing more bullshit! If I said don't call or see that nigga, then I expect you to fucking listen to me! What type of games you playing with me, Normani?" he asked angrily.

Normani cleared her throat. She watched Azariah advance on her car, and his masculine beauty took all her fucking attention. She immediately regretted picking up Tru's call.

"It's too early to be bickering with you about inconsequential bullshit. Have fun in Miami, and we'll see you when you get home. I have to go," Normani said and ended the call.

Tru hit her line repeatedly as she grabbed her daughter and exited her car.

"Watch out, ma. I got her," Azariah said walking up.

Normani stepped to the side and allowed him to pick her sleeping daughter up. She grabbed River's diaper bag and shut the car door before following him into his condo.

"She getting big as hell. I'm missing all this shit with her fucking round with you and that nigga Tru," Azariah grumbled laying River down onto his brown suede and leather sofa.

Normani ignored his remarks as she scanned his new living quarters. Azariah's placed wreaked of cheap perfume, and it killed her. Normani had no grounds to be upset still she was. She slipped off her black and white Vans and cleared her throat.

"Who you have over here that wears Dollar Tree perfume? Let me find out you slumming it up AZ," she half-joked.

Azariah chuckled as he sat down on his loveseat. He grabbed the remote and placed his ochre-hued eyes on her. Azariah

115

had the kind of sexiness that should have been bottled up. Smooth

peanut butter brown skin with detailed tattoos that graced his neck,

chest, and back. Even a few going across the sides of his stomach.

He bore a square-shaped face with a chiseled jaw and full lips.

Azariah rocked his hair in a temple fade and even while he wore his

suits, he kept a diamond in his left ear.

"You," he jested, and she flipped him off while smirking.

Azariah nodded with his eyes pinned to her.

"Keep doing that and I'ma see if you really bout that life," he

said with all playfulness gone from his deep tone.

Normani and Azariah shared an intense staring match until

she looked away. He chuckled as she took a seat beside him.

"Like I thought. What's been up?" he asked unbuttoning his

shirt.

Normani watched Azariah closely as he took off his suit

jacket then his shirt. He relaxed on the sofa, and she couldn't help

but gaze at his tatted chest. Her mouth watered as she envisioned

herself licking on his nipples.

"What I just tell you bout that shit? Don't come over here staring at a nigga unless you ready for me. How you doing? What happened to you coming over the other day?"

Normani took one last glance at his ripped body before clearing her throat.

"Tru overheard us talking that night and was tripping on me hard for a few days. I wasn't in the mood to keep arguing with him, so I waited for him to leave town before coming by. I did something significant today, however."

Azariah nodded. His hand found Normani's thigh, and gently he massaged it while staring at her.

"What's that?" he asked lowly. He held his hand up in the air and leaned towards Normani. Azariah grabbed her bag and set it on her lap. "Put your glasses on, ma. I can see your ass squinting and shit. Gone fuck around and start having migraines from doing that. It's not related to having hemicrania, but you know your pops suffered from them. Just wear the fucking glasses," he complained.

Normani waved Azariah off as she retrieved her glasses from her bag. As she pulled them out of the case, Azariah started to rub on her leg again.

"Now what did you do today besides finally coming to see me?" he asked.

Normani smiled. He was moody with her, but she didn't mind. With Azariah, she never had to question his intentions. His actions always came from a place of love.

"I enrolled in school again. Nothing major just OCC but I'm thrilled to be going back. I have to work something out with River, but I will figure it out. I plan on getting both degrees in half the time. I also hooked back up with one of my friends from, and she's helping me put together a program for River and babies like her. I show parents how to set up their kids for early education," she talked excitedly.

Azariah stopped rubbing her leg to grin at her. He caught Normani off guard when he pulled her into his arms.

"I haven't heard you sound excited like this in a while now. Congrats ma," he said into her neck.

Normani closed her eyes as her thoughts went from school to Azariah. She swallowed hard as his strong hands began to caress her back.

"And I missed you. I missed your pretty ass a lot. Did you miss me?" he asked.

His tone was low, and as he pulled back to stare into her eyes, he smirked at her. Azariah adjusted her frames and shook his head.

"These fucking glasses look sexy as fuck on you. Close your eyes," he told her.

Normani cleared her throat.

"Why?" she asked in a breathy tone.

Azariah chuckled.

"Cause I wanna kiss you and you acting scary as shit so I thought you closing your eyes would make it better. Now can you please close your eyes for me so I can kiss on them soft ass lips you got?"

Normani stared at Azariah for a few moments before doing as he'd instructed. She counted the seconds in her head, and when she got to ten, his thick lips were pressing against her's. Azariah's hand caressed her small breast as his tongue slid into her mouth.

Normani could feel her sex ache as he sucked on her bottom lip.

"Oh," she moaned as her eyes rolled into the back of her head.

"Damn I wanna taste you. Can I?"

Normani shook her head trying to be true to a man that probably wasn't true to her.

"We shouldn't," she murmured pushing him away.

Azariah cupped Normani's face as she stared into his eyes.

"I'ma chill out but tell me, ma. Is any of it still there?"

Normani closed her eyes to calm her racing heart.

"Is any of what still there?"

Azariah kissed her lips again, and she moaned.

"The love you felt for me or did you give it all to that hoe ass nigga?"

His question made her swallow hard. She nodded as she opened her eyes and he let her face go.

"I told you that I still love you and I do. That's not ever changing, but I am with Tru. We have a family together and a life. Still, I don't see why we can't be friends. At least try to see if we can have a friendship," she replied.

Azariah sat back and gritted his teeth. He stared straight ahead as Normani glanced over at her peacefully sleeping baby.

"It feels good to be back. Business with my family is going good, and I'm making a lot of money. But I will say that coming home hurts. I stayed away for so long because of this bullshit. We never had sex but what we have isn't on no friendly shit. I might have played along so that we could keep in touch, but I don't wanna be your damn friend, and you know that."

Normani nodded. She rested against the sofa as she peered over at Azariah.

"You mean something to me AZ, but I am with Tru," she told him.

Azariah looked at Normani and licked his thick lips. His eyes peered into her intently as he grabbed her hand.

"Then friends it is. Just don't expect me to drop everything for you when he not acting right. Remember that I'm your friend. Not your side nigga or backup guy. Just a friend," he replied and turned on the TV.

Normani sighed and scooted over on the sofa. As she rested her head on Azariah's body, he playfully pushed her away. She glanced up at him, and he chuckled.

"Already your ass is blurring the lines. You don't know what the fuck you want," he joked, but his words couldn't be more true for Normani.

With Azariah being home, she felt relief. She was at peace, and that scared her because the feelings he evoked out of her were feelings that Tru should have been giving her.

4

#noneedtoask

The soft cries of the infant made Novah smile. She never thought she would say it, but at times she missed her twins being babies. Now they were little boys acting as if they were grown, men. A lot of their behavior was due to the man that was their father.

Her eyes roamed over the comfortable, clean, sleek family room and she licked her lips.

"I love how you kept the housekeeper and nanny around for Palmer. How is she?"

Arquez, Novah's first cousin looked up from his newborn son. Pride and happiness showed on his handsome face. Arquez doted on his toddler daughter Chanel, and Novah knew that he would spoil this child rotten as well. Much like he did their beautiful mother, Palmer. He'd done unthinkable things to be with Palmer, and their story was one for the books. They had a connection that Novah longed for.

A love Novah couldn't wait to have.

"Palmer gives me everything that a wife should. Even before we said I do, I wanted her to have everything. If I could provide it, I did. I don't want my woman worrying about bullshit like washing clothes and cooking. She needs to be concerned with the kids and me. I'm lucky enough to give it to her like that. How you been? I saw you online the other day and shit. I know you hate how them niggas stalk your every move," he replied.

Novah relaxed on the suede sectional. She hated it as well but was sadly used to it. For the most part, she lived a private life, but whenever she was going through it with Carter, their business somehow made it to the public.

"I'm tired Quez. I know you wanted to hit up the gun range the other day, but I didn't have it in me to go. This whole thing with court has me worried. I don't want to split custody of my kids with him," Novah replied. She looked her cousin in his light shaded eyes and watched his face tighten with anger. "Don't be upset either. If you jump on him, he will call the cops. You know how he is," she told him.

Arquez nodded with a scowl marring his face. Arquez's sister passed away years ago, and from there Novah and him grew close.

Although Arquez distanced himself from the family because of issues with his father, that was Novah's mothers only brother they still kept in contact. They both mourned the death of his sister together, and they were now like brother and sister. Arquez was a protector and wanted badly to defend Novah. Novah, however, was trying to keep the peace. Her cousin placing hands on Carter would only cause more drama. Something she didn't need.

"Look it's like this. My pops is gone, and so is yours. We all we got. If he comes at you on some bitch shit, I'ma take care of it. As my own man, I can't have that shit. No disrespect but fuck your lawyer. I got somebody that can get that nigga together. I already told auntie, and she's cool with it. Just relax and take care of your little dudes. You a good ass mom Novah. If you feel like your kids don't need to be around that ugly bitch like that, then they don't. They're your fucking sons. Fuck the bullshit," Arquez replied before rocking his son who was sleeping peacefully in his arms.

"But in a peaceful way baby. She doesn't need you pulling old Quez out of the closet," Palmer said walking in slowly.

Novah's face lit up at the sound of Palmer's light voice. She stood and quickly embraced her cousin-in-law. Like always Palmer was looking flawless in her leggings that she'd paired with an off the shoulder tee and

125

slippers. Palmer grinned at Novah before they both sat down. Novah watched Arquez's eyes slowly soak in his wife Palmer's appearance before he leaned over. He kissed her tenderly before staring into her eyes.

"Why you out of bed? You hungry I'll have some food brought up to you, ma. Didn't daddy say get your rest?" he asked quietly.

Palmer blushed, and her eyes skated over to Novah. She waved her head playfully and smiled.

"This demanding man. I can't pee without him talking mess. How are the boys? I miss them," Palmer said to her.

Arquez kissed Palmer's cheek, and Novah sighed. She couldn't fucking wait for her soulmate to find her. She could only pray he was on the way.

"They're good. They're actually at football practice right now. You know Carter has them in all these programs. Programs that he's not even paying for, but it's cool. I make it work. For them I always will," she replied.

"I'ma get at that nigga," Arquez grumbled, and Palmer rubbed his leg lovingly.

"Relax baby. Not all men are like you. Not every man does right by their woman or the mother of their kids. He will have to learn that a hard head makes a soft ass," Palmer said calmly, and Novah couldn't help but to laugh.

"You been around your man way too long. But I need to get out of here. I just came by to see the newest Royale. You all are giving me baby fever, and I don't even have a man."

Palmer smiled as Arquez stared up at Novah. His slanted light eyes regarded her intently as she pulled her fob from her Chloe bag.

"I'm serious though cousin. It's nothing I won't do for the women I love. I'm out the streets, but that shit will always be in a nigga. I'm coming with you to every court date, and I want his bitch ass to say something out of pocket. We don't play that shit round here. The only reason I haven't pulled up on him yet is cause of my lil dudes, but he's reaching now. Got me wanting to find his ass."

Novah nodded as she swallowed hard. Carter was playing games because that was him. He was nothing but a bullshitter, but the thing was Novah had real killers on speed dial. Niggas that did no talking and she prayed that Carter didn't make her cousin revert back to his old ways. She knew that for her he would.

Novah walked over to Arquez and leaned down. She kissed his cheek before kissing the baby's forehead. She then smiled at Palmer.

"Don't worry about me. I'm good. I can handle whatever he throws my way Quez and the minute I can't I'll call you."

She stood up, and Arquez frowned up at her.

"I'm serious. I don't like the way shit it's looking with this nigga. If he gets out of line, let me know. It's nothing for Tarik and me to pull up on his ass. Okay?"

Novah nodded. She knew that her cousin was upset with the situation and that warmed her heart. With her father being gone it felt good to know that she had male figures in her life that were concerned with her wellbeing.

"I'm serious the second he gets out of pocket with me. I will let you know," she said to soothe her cousins' mind.

Carter had fucking been out of pocket with her, but she wouldn't let her family know that.

"Now I really gotta go. I'll see you all later, and the baby is so handsome it's insane. Love you all!"

"We love you too!" Palmer yelled back as Novah briskly left the family room.

Novah exited the large home and jumped in her truck. After checking the time, she sped to her son's game. Arriving ten minutes late she pulled into an available spot and was shocked to see Carter's white Wraith in the parking lot. Usually, his mother dropped them off at the Saturday games if she couldn't.

Carter was only hands-on when it benefited him, unfortunately.

Instantly a queasy feeling entered Novah at the thought of him being at the game. Nothing ever good came from her interactions with him, and her patience with his disrespect had run so thin it was barely there.

"Here we go," she muttered while placing on her baseball cap.

Novah then exited her truck and pulled up her high waisted skinny jeans before heading into the building. Loud ruckus, kids laughing, and chatter greeted her as she entered the building. Much like it always was when she came in contact with the other sex, the men immediately zoned in on her. The whitewash jeans hugged her meaty thighs and small waist. The white top that bore her son's jersey numbers showed off her 40

C cup breast, and with every step she took they bounced despite the bra attempting to hold them in.

She licked her lips as she headed for the bleachers to the right of the room. The indoor faux football field was perfect for future ballers. Novah's twins had been attending for the last six months, and while it was high as shit, they loved it, so she always found a way to pay for the $1200 monthly tuition.

"Hey, girl! The boys are on it today," Laurie another football mom said as Novah took a seat.

Novah nodded as she ignored the intense glare from Carters wife that sat two rows up. With Novah, pregnancy enhanced her features. Brought out the glow to her mocha shaded skin. Made her already big ass nicer and had her breast even juicier. With Melanie, it wasn't quite the same. Bad acne marks covered her face while her nose spread to unnatural levels. She wore a look of bitterness on her round face that made Novah smirk. While Novah wore clothing that molded to her frame, Melanie wore Fendi spandex shorts with a sports bra and the matching jacket. Melanie had even gone as far as to wear the logo cap, and to Novah she looked dumb as shit. For several reasons but the most significant one being she was at a kid's football game. Not the club or the bar and the outfit didn't look good on her.

Novah snickered at how silly Melanie looked, and Laurie smiled.

"It don't come easy for everybody," Laurie muttered making Novah laugh.

Melanie sat up and rolled her neck.

"What's so funny? I wanna laugh too," she said sliding down a bench.

"Then look in the fucking mirror," Novah murmured, and Laurie covered her mouth to laugh.

"What the fuck did you just say!" Melanie asked loudly making people glance their way.

Novah smiled as she crossed her legs and stared at her boys on the field. Melanie was all bark and no bite. Years of run-ins with the woman had shown her that.

"Calm down girl. You're pregnant," Laurie told her glancing back at Melanie.

Melanie rolled her eyes at Laurie.

"And you're in some business that's not your fucking own. I'm not Carter, Novah. You don't want to play with me. Pregnant or not shit will get real for your ass," Melanie said as Carter walked over with the coach.

Melanie sat back and smiled as Carter advanced on them. Novah's mocha shaded skin burned as she struggled to keep her composure. Doing the right thing wasn't always easy. Melanie was a real bitch, and Novah was itching to read the fuck out of her.

"I'd love to see that," Novah said quietly to Melanie as Carter took a seat beside her.

Melanie snorted and laughed lightly. She leaned on Carter's arm as Novah watched her boys stand on the field.

"Oh, you will when we make it to court sweetie. Life will change for your stuck-up ass real quick then. No more partying on my man. No more trips on us boo-boo. You'll actually have to put some work in at that dingy ass spa," Melanie retorted loudly.

Novah attempted to glance back at Melanie and Laurie pulled on her arm.

"Ignore them. He's on his way to ruining his career, and she's ugly," Laurie whispered pulling Novah closer to her.

Novah sighed, even smiled briefly at Laurie's attempt to make her relax. She bit down hard on her bottom lip as she replayed the nasty things Melanie had spoken to her. Carter and his wife didn't know when to quit. They were the kind of people that couldn't stop themselves from poking a sleeping bear.

Just dumb as fuck for no reason.

"Chill out with all that. Let her act ratchet on her own baby. Her ass don't have no home training. You know she's thirsty for attention and shit. You better than that. Plus, I don't want these motherfucka's in my business," Carter said silencing Melanie.

Irritated with the situation Novah began to bounce her leg to keep from cursing Carter and his wife out. Seconds later the game started back up, and it brought a big smile to Novah's face. Within minutes King took the football from the other toddler team and raced down the field. Happiness coursed through Novah as she jumped up and down for her baby. He was as good as his father and Novah was glad to see Carter pass something good down to their sons.

"Yes, King! You got it baby!" she shouted like a proud mom.

"Why your ass so fat?" Carter whispered lowly making Novah jump.

He chuckled as she glared back at him. Novah looked back to where Melanie had just been sitting, and Carter shook his head.

"She went to go call her mom back. Why you always looking for her?" he asked.

Novah's eyes scanned over his clean, nice appearance and still, she saw the ugliness in him. The Polo outfit, designer shoes, and fresh haircut couldn't mask the ugliness brewing inside of him.

"Because you're constantly acting like you forgot about her," she quipped before looking back at the game.

Novah ignored Carter as the kids continued to play. Carter slid beside Novah, and his hand fell to her waist. He gripped it tightly as she ignored his presence.

"All this shit can stop if you agree to the days. I don't wanna take you to court, and I know you don't wanna go. Why you bugging out on a nigga like this? I mean do you think I would let her harm my kids?" he asked.

Novah discreetly pulled away from Carter. She noticed a few people stare their way and she shook her head.

"Carter this is not the place to discuss this. I don't even want you over here near me right now. You were just talking shit about me two seconds ago."

Carter placed his hand at the small of her back as he leaned towards her.

"You get to playing roles, so I play them bitches right along with you. We not together because your ass left. Don't get mad that I'm with Melanie. Shit, she was there for me. She still is, but we both know who I love. If you done playing games then I'll let her ass go," he said quietly.

Novah's face scrunched up as she watched her sons run up and down the field. Carter was so insane with his antics that he was surprising even her with his selfish words.

"Wow, you don't give a fuck about anyone but yourself. I don't want you. Shit, why would I want the man that's hitting on his ex-woman while he's with his pregnant wife? What can you possibly bring into my life besides more drama Carter?"

"Carter, what the fuck is going on?"

Novah and Carter looked back at Melanie as she held two hotdogs and a bottled water. Carter took his time removing his hand from Novah's back, and Novah shook her head.

Couldn't be her.

"We were discussing the court shit. You good baby? And did you get me something to eat?" he asked going back to Melanie's side.

Melanie's angry eyes bored into Novah as she slowly sat down.

"I'm his wife," she said evenly and held her head up high while flashing Novah her dazzling wedding ring.

The same ring that Carter had tried to give to Novah when he'd been caught cheating with Melanie years ago.

Novah nodded while holding in her laugh. Melanie couldn't hurt her feelings because she knew the truth. Melanie had her position by default. She was merely Carter's number one girl because no other woman including Novah stuck around for his shit. Novah glanced over at Carter who was staring a hole into her before looking back to Melanie.

"Then you should remind your husband of that."

As Novah sat down, Melanie and Carter began to argue. Laurie glanced over at Novah and shook her head.

"He's a piece of shit. How do you deal with him?" she asked.

Laurie was married to an NFL player as well. She'd met Novah through Carter who was her husbands' friend at the time. That friendship was now over. However, Laurie kept in contact with Novah.

"I don't. You see how I was ignoring him? That's me most of the time. The shit he says goes in one ear and out the other. I don't have time for it, you know?"

Laurie nodded with empathetic eyes. She pulled Novah to her side and playfully kissed her cheek.

"My mother once told me that nothing was in vain. The problems Carter put you through will only make you stronger. Your pain, your tears none of it will be for nothing. A good man is coming, and when he gets to you, men like Carter will make you appreciate him so much more. Just watch," Laurie told her.

Novah nodded with a small smile on her face.

"I'ma hold your momma to that," Novah said quietly making Laurie and herself snicker.

House note: 1800

Dominique Thomas
Kids daycare: 2000

Football: 1200

Spa mortgage: 1100

Novah stopped jotting down her bills to look up at her best friend. Billie had started out her nemesis. They'd both been vying for the same skinny ass boy in grade school. He'd dated both of them even kissed Novah in between classes which made her feel extra special. Once word spread that they were both his girlfriend they were ready to fight. Novah and Billie met up in the locker room and battled it out. Fought hard for the boy that was playing both of them. In the end, they were both dumped by him for the sixth grader that was giving it up.

While dealing with their first heartbreak, they became friends. They now laughed at the silly ass story, but they wouldn't change a thing about it. Silas with the big nose and handsome face had brought them together.

Billie sat the Allure Boutique bags down onto the black marble top counter and grinned at Novah.

"I'm here. I'm coming to the rescue," she told her.

Novah sat her pen down and gave her girl a once over. Billie like always was runway ready. She wore a black custom bustier bodycon dress

138

designed by her friend Mickey, and she'd paired the look with Versace

pumps and a small cutch. Billie's dark honey blonde strands were up in a

frilly bun with a few pieces falling in the front. She held a sexy, playful look

to her visage as she stood before Novah.

"You know I always love your presence but did I ask you to come

over? I planned on spending my Friday night in. I need to go over my bills

and see what I can cut down."

Billie smiled. She began to go through the boutique bags while

looking at Novah.

"You didn't have to ask me. I knew you needed your friend. My

best friend antenna's been going off all damn week. I could feel that a

night out was coming so here I am. We have both been tired and stressed

out, but for tonight none of our problems will exist. No Carter and no

Malachi. That's the first and last time I'll even speak they bitch ass

names," Billie replied.

Novah smiled. She wanted to protest, but Billie was right. They

needed a night out. Shit, they deserved one.

"But are you cool with the club vibe?" Novah asked her girl.

Billie had been clean, and she didn't see it changing anytime soon

but like always she wanted to be supportive of her friend. Novah never wanted to place her best friend in a position that would set her back. Going to the club wasn't that damn important.

"I mean we can stay in and order movies," she suggested.

Billie waved her off.

"It's not actually a club. It's an upscale penthouse party. Like the who's who of Michigan and shit but I was invited, nonetheless. It's a chill vibe, and people don't be on that fake flossing shit, so you don't have to worry about photos of us popping up online," Billie assured her.

Novah nodded. That was like music to her ears. She loved to be in the moment and relax. She didn't want to have to look over her shoulder all night for the lurkers.

"Okay, cool. So, what you bring me?"

Billie laughed. She laid out the dresses for Novah and like a kid in the candy store Novah rushed over to the counter to look them over.

"Mickey is too damn talented! I can't wait for the world to get up on her," Novah gushed.

Billie nodded while smiling.

"I know, and she's going to get her shine eventually. She's too talented not to. What you want to wear?"

Novah nibbled on her bottom lip as she looked the precious threads over. Her eyes zeroed in on the peachy latex nude spaghetti strap dress, and her heart raced. It had been a while since she'd been grown and sexy. Life had been pulling her in every direction and mommy mode was all she seemed to be in at the moment. She grabbed the dress and Billie whistled.

"Honey that ass bout to be popping out the dress," Billie raved.

Novah laughed. She wanted a drink, but because she was mindful of her girl, she chose to not pop the liquor out in front of her. Billie assured her repeatedly that she was good, but Novah didn't want to tempt her.

"I'ma do this one," Novah murmured holding the dress close to her chest.

"Then let's get you ready," Billie said and pulled her away.

After showering and curling her long thick mane into loose curls, Novah sat at her vanity as Billie applied her makeup. The dress like expected stuck to her curvy body like it was second skin. Novah felt sexy as she stared up at her girl.

"I haven't seen you in days. What kind of BF are you?" Novah asked Billie.

Billie laughed as she put Novah's long mink lashes on.

"Well, I've been working boo. I did a shoot for Mickey, and I took another job that was in New York. I was reluctant to get back out there, but it feels right. Modeling is a huge part of me, and I can't fight that. I've also been with my new sponsor. She's a college student that's trying to kick liquor, and I know she can."

Novah grinned up at her girl. Billie had the kind of beauty that intimidated a lot of people, but the thing was her outer appearance didn't have shit on her inner beauty. Billie was a pure soul, and Novah was relieved that she was over her storm.

"With you by her side, she can't go wrong. How is it in loversville? You know I 'm not getting any dick. It's been a year for me," Novah pouted.

Billie gasped dramatically, and Novah hit her leg.

"Don't front like you didn't know now spill it. How is your future husband Dreux doing?"

Billie's face lit up at the mention of her man.

"He's good. Amazing like always. He took me to the DeLoines hotel to celebrate my sober anniversary. It was really nice."

Novah whistled. The DeLoines hotel was considered the cream of the crop. Compared to the likes of the Four Seasons and it was the nicest five-star hotel that Michigan possessed. Novah hadn't had the pleasure of going before but had always heard such good things about the place.

"Oh, you had to bust it open for him real good that night. I heard that place was like $600 a night and that's for the standard room. Does Fat Albert know about him yet?"

Billie snorted before falling into a fit of laughter. Novah joined in with her, and they both had a good laugh at Malachi's expense.

"Hell no! And tonight, we will not speak about them fuck niggas. It's about us and having a good time nothing more," Billie replied.

Novah nodded as she stared up at her friend.

"I will say this, and we will be done with it. The whole Malachi and Dreux thing is messed up, but I honestly feel like if anyone was to be mad, it should be Dreux. You was his, and we all knew that you all liked each other. Even Malachi. That's why he was so happy when Dreux went away to college. It was then that his ass started hating on Dreux. Telling you about Kylie and all that bullshit to get you onto his side. You never cared for Malachi though, and I'm still clueless as to how you fucked him because when I left from his place, you weren't that drunk Billie."

There was an uncomfortable silence as Billie finished up Novah's makeup. Once she was done, she gave her a tight-lipped smile.

"All done. Let's go," she said and briskly exited the room.

Novah sighed wishing her girl would stand up to her baby daddy. She wasn't judging because she was constantly dealing with Carter's bullshit, but she did want Billie would stand up to Malachi. Novah ignored Carter, but she wasn't afraid of him. Novah feared that her girl was scared of Malachi and that was what pissed her off the most. Malachi was a weak ass nigga, and Novah was sure that he did play a hand in Billie getting intoxicated enough to fuck him but if Billie wanted to leave it buried then for her friend she would.

Uptown, nigga

I was down, but they see, I'm up now, nigga

Head high 'cause I'm holdin' up my crown, nigga

Never told even through the ups and downs, nigga

And if I D'usse, it's a cup of brown, nigga

The vibe inside the luxury apartment was chill. Billie talked with a fellow model friend as Novah nursed a glass of wine. She'd insisted on not drinking, and Billie begged her to get a glass. Novah reluctantly took it and was enjoying herself enough to be happy she'd stepped out of the house.

Detroit's elite was what Billie dubbed the crowd to be, and boy was she right. Local rappers, models, and actors even hood celebrities and local socialites partied in the swagged out apartment that took up the entire twentieth floor. Novah sat beside Billie quietly when a familiar sexy ass face grabbed her attention.

Like he was before Durand stood out in the crowd of handsome, wealthy young black men. The diamonds around his neck sparkled with every move he made as he laughed at what his fellow groupmate Malano said to him.

Novah swallowed hard and chose to drain her glass of wine. Her honey colored eyes roamed deliberately over Durand as he stood a few feet away from her. He wore white jeans that were tattered by the knees with a white crew neck and multi-colored Chanel sneakers. A multi-colored Chanel rag was folded and tied around his head while Bugatti shades covered his eyes. His jewelry was simple but shined effortlessly as it covered his wrist, left ear, and left pinky finger.

When Durand laughed, Novah was able to see his pearly white teeth. She marveled at how straight and pretty they were. Her teeth sunk into her bottom lip as she fantasized about the attractive rapper.

"Eye spy with my little eye a sexy ass rapper that you need to be getting on. Hey Durand!" Billie called out and waved at him.

Novah immediately stopped lusting over the man and looked the other way. Suddenly her bladder became full, and she found herself standing.

"I see Novah still shutting shit down," Shyy another local rapper noted staring over at her.

Novah smiled at the young, handsome rapper before glaring at her best friend.

"What? And I hope you know he staring at that big old ass you got," Billie said giddily.

Novah whimpered. She rolled her eyes and briskly walked out of the living room. Her eyes scanned the long hallway before a warm, rough hand grabbed her arm.

"It's this way."

The thick timber of his voice made the fine hairs on her body stand to attention. Novah took a deep breath and exhaled. The last thing she wanted to do was come off as a groupie. Years ago, rappers were like regular people to her. She'd partied hard with the best of them, but for some reason, Durand was unnerving her.

"Thanks," she managed to croak out.

Durand let her arm go and made her heart pump faster when he grabbed her hand.

"I'll take you."

Novah swallowed hard.

"I didn't need for you to do that. I could have found it."

"I'm the kind of nigga that gives you what you need before you even have to ask for it. It's right up here," he remarked and led her down the hallway.

Novah's legs felt like they weighed a ton as she walked with Durand down the narrow hallway. As they went further away from the party, Novah began to spot plaques on the wall. Durand's rap group's name was plastered on everyone making her raise her brows.

"Is this your home?"

Durand glanced over at her and smiled.

"If I say yes what do I get?"

Novah laughed off his question. Slowly her nervousness was waning away.

"Whatever you want," she said sultrily.

Durand grinned before looking ahead.

"Yeah okay but yes this my spot. I must admit I'm shocked to see you here. We been in the industry together for years and never ran into each other."

Novah nodded.

"Yes, and I'm not in the industry. I was just a video model," she clarified.

Durand stopped at the guest bathroom and removed his shades. His intense eyes stared down at Novah in a way that made her nerves vibrate with anticipation.

"Video models is a part of the culture. Shit, all the memorable ones are, and you definitely is an OG. I realized that at the spa, but I didn't wanna say shit to make you upset. Some women get mad when you ask them about, they younger days and shit."

Novah's jaw fell slack, and she playfully hit Durand's arm.

"Younger years? Nigga, I'm thirty. I'm still young," she boasted.

Durand nodded while staring down at her.

"I'm just fucking with you. You only five years older than me. You at the perfect age and shit. Jay been said thirty was the new twenty," he replied.

Novah waved him off, and he chuckled.

"Don't use Jay to get me back on your good side," she replied.

Durand grabbed her hand and pulled her close to him. His scent assaulted her head on and for the first time since she'd been in his presence, she allowed for it to place a spell on her. Her nostrils breathed in the cashmere musk scent, and Durand leaned down.

"As long as I'm on any side of you, I'm good. I want you to use the bathroom then have a drink with me. That's cool?" he asked.

Novah stared up into his eyes with her mind racing.

"One drink is fine," she whispered.

Durand smiled. He nodded and took a step back.

"Cool, then I'll be right here waiting on you."

Novah nodded and turned around. She quickly went into the bathroom and relieved her bladder. Several seconds after finishing Novah sat on the toilet lost in her thoughts.

Durand was fine, like fine as fuck. Charming she could tell from their brief encounter, and he had her wanting to act bad for the night, but could she? How would he view her if she did? Novah hadn't pulled out her inner freak in years. The twins had calmed her spirit and her hot pussy down. She now craved quietness. Looked forward to going to bed at nine every night and was simply put boring as fuck.

For one night only she wanted to be the old Novah. The Novah that wasn't stressing about Carter. The Novah that didn't have the world on her shoulders. She wanted to let her hair down and just go with the flow.

"If he asks I'ma say yes. I deserve some fun..." Novah stopped whispering and shook her head. "No fuck that I deserve some dick. Every woman deserves to get her back blown out at least once a damn year and the lucky ones get it regularly."

Novah snickered at her silliness before flushing the toilet. She wiped herself and quickly washed her hands. Novah stared at her beautiful face in the mirror and smiled. She felt sexy. The bouncy curls gave her the look along with the sleek makeup Billie had applied. Novah dropped her head and fluffed her curls. She tossed her head back at the sexy bedhead hair she was blessed with made her smile wider. Novah bit down on her bottom lip as she nodded.

"Get his lil sexy ass," she murmured before exiting the bathroom.

Durand stood on the other end of the bathroom door against the wall. His eyes peered up from the ground and across at Novah. The intense look his dark peepers placed on her made her confidence dwindle, but it didn't dissipate. No Novah shook her nerves off and grinned at him sexily.

"You ready?" she asked quietly.

Durand nodded while staring down at her. His hand went to the back of his neck, and he rubbed it while gazing at her.

"I should be asking you that. You smoke?"

Novah nodded then quickly shook her head then she nodded again. Durand chuckled at her indecisiveness.

"Well I used to then I had kids, so I stopped, but I didn't stop liking the weed. I just chose mommy hood over getting high. You know?"

Durand grabbed Novah's hand and pulled her close to him.

"I think you can have both. Come fuck with me," he said and pulled her away.

Novah walked silently beside Durand as they reentered the partying side of the apartment. They bypassed a talkative Billie that discreetly gave Novah a cheesy thumbs up and walked into the lounge room. The lights were dimmed, but it was still filled to the brim with people. Durand found an available seat on his L-shaped suede sectional and pulled Novah onto his lap. Novah tried to stand up not liking the attention they garnered from his personal move, and he leaned towards her ear.

"These my people, relax. This not no industry shit. Is it?" he asked and peered around at the people flanking the room.

Everyone shook their heads before going back to their conversations. Novah relaxed when she noticed no one was in their grill and Durand pulled weed from his pocket. He chose to roll up on Novah's lap as she listened to the music playing in the room.

"So, tell me some shit bout you that the media doesn't know," he said pulling her away from her thoughts.

Novah relaxed more into his broad chest and sighed. This was the closest she'd been to a man in months, and she was close to creaming her thongs from his deep voice alone.

"I'm a sweetheart," her light voice replied making him chuckle.

"Is that right? Would your old nigga say the same thing?"

Novah shrugged. Carter was miles away to her. For the night, his bitch ass didn't exist.

"Please pretend he doesn't exist," she murmured as the song switched to another track.

Durand breathed harder, and his warm breath fanned Novah's neck. Her eyes closed briefly, and he finished up rolling his blunt.

"I understand. Although I don't have any kids, I can tell shit can get hectic when you beefing with the person you made a kid with. Can I ask you a question though?"

Novah nodded. She opened her eyes and spotted another rapper, Durand's groupmate Trill staring at them. He shot her a playful smirk before leaving out of the room.

"What made you have a kid with somebody that you don't wanna even speak of now? I could never see myself doing something like that.

That's why I'm watchful with the dick, and I always strap up. My wife, the only person, having my kids and the woman I marry will be my fucking soulmate. We gone connect naturally and we'll know from the start that we meant to be together," Durand stopped talking and chuckled lowly. "I know this shit sound crazy, but it's real. I'm not procreating with just anybody. I watch people go through meaningless drama all because they had a kid with somebody that they don't even fucking like. Shit is crazy to me," he grumbled.

Durand lit up the blunt as Novah processed his words. Novah gingerly slid off his lap and turned to him. She kicked off her heels wanting her feet to get a break and Durand's intense gaze shifted her way. She watched him inspect her toes before licking his lips.

"You mad about what I said?"

Novah shook her head. She was lowkey pissed but lied not to show her pettiness.

"I hate when people assume. People lie daily. You can meet someone, and they can pretend to be everything you ever wanted in a person. They can be perfect for you until you're so deep into love with them that when the real them comes out, it's too late. Years have gone by, you've built a life with this person, and now you have kids with them.

154

Nothing is ever what it seems Durand. I didn't fuck Carter because he had money. I had money then, and I have money now. I never needed for no man to fucking take care of me. If I wanted that I could be with a million men getting their money. I'm different though. I always wanted to be more than a pretty face. I used the video modeling money to buy a spa. I turned that into something that I could give my kids if they wanted it. Yes, it's stressful, but it brings in great consistent money. I'm hoping to open another one in a few months. But back to Carter, he was different in the beginning."

Durand blew weed smoke from between his thick lips and stared at Novah.

"Was he though or did you see only what you wanted to see? So many women will make a dog ass nigga the man of their dreams because he a good look for them. They'll pass up the garbage man and post office working nigga for the hustler. Or for the blue collared nigga and get fucking dragged in the end. People show you even when they hiding it who they are. He gave away signs in the beginning ma, trust you just missed them," he told her.

Durand passed Novah the blunt, and she took it as her eyes narrowed to slits.

"Don't shoot the messenger beautiful. I'm blunt, and if you can't take that, then our friendship won't make it."

Novah hit the blunt twice before passing it back to Durand.

"Who said I wanted to be your fucking friend?"

Durand chuckled. He leaned towards Novah and his lips brushed against her cheek before he whispered in her ear, "That wet pussy that you got is telling me that. I can smell you from here and not in a bad way. In a way that so good, it's got me wanting to take you to the back," he revealed.

Novah swallowed hard and looked away from Durand.

He kissed her neck before sitting back. Quietly they finished the blunt together, and an hour later Billie walked into the room all smiles. She advanced on Novah as Durand massaged Novah's foot.

"Novah, you ready or you staying the night?" she joked before yawning.

Novah's relaxed body that was sedated under the influence of the loud Sativa strain had her smiling. She stared up at her girl all smiles, and Billie laughed lightly. Billie leaned down and kissed Novah's forehead.

"You sure?"

Novah's eyes connected with Durand's and he licked his lips. He applied pressure to the ball of her foot, and a light moan escaped her lips. If he had her foot feeling so well how would he handle the rest of her body?

"Umm...yeah. I'm good."

Billie nodded. She looked to Durand, and he smirked up at her.

"Aye, you know how far we go back. I been asking you about this beautiful ass woman. Don't front like you ain't know," he said to her.

Billie narrowed her eyes as she placed her hand on her hip.

"For this one here I will go First 48 crazy on your ass. A piece of my heart is in your possession. Don't fuck it up," she warned him.

Durand nodded.

"I won't, and I respect that. She's in good hands," he said sincerely.

Billie stared at Durand a little longer before nodding. She smiled at Novah and winked.

"Call me and if it's any problems definitely call and let me know," she said before walking off.

Novah watched her girl exit the room before looking back to Durand. Slowly his hand went from rubbing her foot to sliding up her right leg. Novah's eyes darted around the room, and she realized that they were nearly alone. A couple sat in the front of the lounge lost in their own conversation. Novah looked back at Durand, and he licked his lips.

"I wanna tell you some shit bout me. If you don't like it, I'll take you home. If you do like it, we can really have some fun. Okay?"

Novah's heartbeat increased. She slowly nodded, and his hand slid further. It rested under her dress and in between her thick thighs. She felt him slowly massage her fat vagina lips, and she moaned.

"I like to fuck. Something might be wrong with me. I think bout pussy all fucking day. Like when I saw you at your spa, I thought damn, she beautiful as shit. I wonder how her pussy taste? And let's be clear I don't go around eating pussy like that, but you got me curious. Then you turned around and..." Durand stopped talking and slid his fingers to the side of her thongs. Two of them probed at her saturated opening before sliding in. They groaned in unison, and Durand sat up. His fingers ventured deep into her warm canal, and he curved them upwards. "And I wondered, what her ass tastes like? I love everything about a woman. Its niggas that like to get they shit off then there's me. I promise you ain't never met a nigga like me before. I'ma pussy monster. You know what that mean?" he asked fucking her hard with his fingers.

Novah's eyes shot to the front of the lounge, and the couple in the room continued to talk oblivious to the pleasure mounting from the back of the room.

Novah shook her head as her thighs began to shake. Durand pumped his fingers harder into her, and she whimpered. It was taking everything in her to keep quiet.

"I come through, and I kill pussy. Murder that shit. Make it hard for you to do anything without thinking about me fucking you, licking you, sucking the cum out of your ass. You think you can handle that?"

Novah stared into Durand's eyes, and he leaned towards her. He bit her bottom lip hard, and seconds later her body fell apart for him.

"Ahhhhhhh," she whimpered as he sexed her with his fingers so roughly, yet so sensually that she climaxed again.

"Shhhh...this ain't shit sexy. Come on. I wanna show you something," he said and pulled his fingers out of her.

Durand helped Novah stand, and she leaned on him as they slowly exited the room. Novah could feel her wetness sliding down her legs as they walked down the hall. Slowly the party was emptying, and the further Durand took her away from the get together the more nervous she became.

Durand took Novah to a door in the back of his apartment on the other end of the floorplan and unlocked it. He pushed it open for Novah, and she walked in. Her eyes soaked in the room as he stepped in behind her.

"Why is it padded?" Novah asked wondering if she was making the wrong decision.

She'd seen things like this, even read about it before but never had she been in a sex room. Thoughts of murder from rough sex began to plague her mind.

"My mom lives with me. I don't want her to hear me getting down and shit," Durand replied casually.

Seconds later the lighting was dimmed, and soft, soulful music began to play in the room. Novah walked over to the swing that sat in the middle of the floor, and she touched the straps.

"I can't fit in this," she murmured.

Durand took off his shirt and chuckled.

"That shit holds up to seven hundred pounds. Trust you good ma. Come here," he demanded.

Novah turned, and her eyes slid over his exposed muscular chest. He wasn't as big as Carter, but still, he was toned up. Tattoos decorated his chest and neck while two quarter sized circles decorated his top pecs. Novah walked over to Durand and touched the marks.

"What happened?"

Durand's hands went to her hips before sliding around to her ample ass. He squeezed it hard, and she groaned. He was so rough.

But she liked it.

"I was shot when I was fourteen for carjacking somebody. I almost died," he revealed lowly

Novah swallowed hard at his revelation.

"I didn't know that," she said quietly.

Durand leaned down, and his lips brushed against her forehead before he kissed her lips. The look he placed on her played tricks with Novah's mind. They were practically strangers. Had only interacted with each other twice yet she felt connected with him. Felt a closeness to him that she hadn't felt before.

"This weed has me tripping," she said and laughed.

Durand nodded.

"You know what we doing right? I don't think you the type, but I don't want no funny style shit in the morning. Do you want this? I need you to verbally tell me yes Novah," he said and began to kiss her neck.

Novah closed her eyes as his lips gave her neck pleasure like never before. Her body relaxed into his as she let go of her inhibitions. Even if only for one night.

"I do. I want it so fucking bad," she admitted.

Durand chuckled. He pulled back and licked his thick lips.

"Good girl. I do too, and now I'm bout to give you what you need. Get naked," he told her and walked off.

Novah's eyes slid across the room once more, and she took off her dress. A large four poster bed sat to the left of the room. To the right was a mini bar and stripper pole. In the middle of the room was the swing and while the walls were a soft ivory color, the carpet was blood red. The room held gold accents of candles and lamps even the drapes were gold.

Novah allowed for her dress to slide to the floor and she yelped when Durand's warm hands slid over her ass.

162

"Get in the swing," he said quietly while still gripping her ample behind.

Novah smiled.

"I need a drink. I'm nervous."

Durand chuckled.

"I got you, but we not gone get drunk. I want you to remember all the shit that's bout to happen," he murmured and led her over to the swing.

Novah allowed for Durand to strap her into the swing and position her legs so that they were opened in a V-shape. Durand made sure Novah was strapped in tightly before standing up. His low lids soaked in her body as he looked at her.

"I've never seen anybody as sexy as you. You beautiful as shit," he revealed before walking over to the bar.

Novah's heart raced as Durand opened the seal on some white liquor. She watched him pour them both a glass and water her drink down with juice. She gave him a nervous grin as he walked back over to her carrying the small glasses.

"I didn't want any juice."

Durand nodded.

"And I don't want you drunk ma. Not tonight maybe next time," he replied.

Quietly they finished the drinks while looking into each other's eyes. Durand then put the glasses away and took off his clothes. As Novah stared down at his large member, he grabbed nipple clamps and a cup of ice.

Durand walked over to Novah and kissed her lips sensually. Novah felt so exposed and bare to him as she peered into his eyes.

"I'm nervous as hell," she admitted lowly.

Durand nodded. He placed the gold nipple clamps onto her hard nipples and ran his free hand through her hair.

"Don't be. If you don't like it just let a nigga know. My only goal is to make you cum until you can't take anymore. Now stick your tongue out," he instructed.

Novah's heart pumped wildly as she did as he'd asked. Durand leaned down to gently suck on her tongue as he shoved a small ice cube up her vagina. Novah's thighs immediately began to shake as the cold cube awakened her sex.

"Relax baby," he whispered pulling back.

Durand dropped down to his knees, and while staring up at Novah, he began to catch the liquid falling from her opening. He pulled on the clamps gently, and Novah cried out.

"Oh God! Damn!" she whimpered.

Durand lapped up her pussy like he was licking a bowl of milk and pulled the clamps harder.

"You like that?"

Novah nodded. He pulled the clamps again this time with more force, and her eyes rolled into the back of her head.

"I do, I do!" she yelled.

Durand zeroed in on her clitoris, and Novah feared she would fall from the swing as her body began to shake. Within a minute she came into Durand's mouth.

Durand licked her clean before standing up. He grabbed an XL magnum and joined her at the swing. After wrapping up his member, he slid his hands up and down her legs that were still aimed up in the air.

"You taste so fucking good. Give me a kiss," he demanded.

Novah swallowed hard and leaned up as much as she could to bless him with her lips. As Durand attacked Novah with his full lips, his dick pushed into her tight walls. Novah tried to pull back to cry out, and he shook his head.

"Don't run. Take it ma," he whispered against her lips.

Novah stared into his alluring eyes as rapture covered her face. Weakly she nodded as her body received pleasure like no other.

"Damn.... shit you feel good," Durand said pulling back. He grabbed Novah's legs, and while staring into her eyes, he commenced to beating her pussy up. Loud cries of pleasure bounced off the walls as he rocked her back and forth on his large penis.

"Oh God! Oh Fuck! Damn! Shit!" Novah cried feeling like a virgin.

Durand moved slightly to the left and Novah's body jerked. She felt him began to knock against an unfamiliar spot inside of her and she grew worried.

"Wait! What the fuck is happening?" she asked while tingling.

Sweat gathered at the top of Durand's brows. He glanced down at his dick as it slid in and out of Novah and he swallowed hard.

"That's what I was looking for ma. Didn't I tell you I was a pussy monster? You thought I was fucking playing? Relax and cum. That's all I want you to do," he replied.

Novah shook her head while trying to pull him closer to her. Tears filled her eyes as her heart raced.

"I can't! Oh God! I can't"! she whined with a tear falling from her eye.

Durand pulled on her nipple clamp and pounded into Novah aggressively. Novah's head fell back and while she cried out at the top of her lungs a fountain of pleasure erupted from her thick frame.

⬚

5

#do4love

9:52 I need to borrow $3000 to fix my car. What's up?

10:30 You ain't shit. I need to use that money for my damn car. That's how our son gets around.

11:00 Aye you gone let me have that shit or not? I been helping my mom with bills and shit is tight for me.

11:30 Fuck you.

11:40 Drunk bitch.

Billie rubbed the crust from her left eye and sighed. Her eyes shifted to Dreux before gazing back to the large cellphone screen. She watched another bubble pop up, and she sighed.

11:42 My bad, I been stressing. I really need this money. Can you do that for me?

Billie's fingers moved quickly against the screen.

Yeah.

11:45 that's what's up. Can you bring it to my job at one?

Billie rolled her eyes. She read over Malachi's earlier texts before responding. Everything in her wanted to text back fuck you, but she didn't. For her son, she would play nice.

Only for him.

Yeah.

She responded instead. Billie put her phone away after clearing out his hateful words. Her eyes ascended to the ceiling as she contemplated on if she should give Malachi the money. He possessed a great job and was paying no rent. His money only went to things of luxury still the guilt of losing her son and knowing that he was with his father made her wanna pay it.

"What's wrong?"

Dreux's warm large hand slid over to Billie and caressed her bare thigh. He squeezed it gently before slipping it between her soft feathery legs. She closed her eyes as he protectively held her velvety mound.

"Nothing."

Dreux sighed. He massaged her lips sensually until wetness seeped from between her opening.

"If you say so beautiful. How you feeling?"

Billie had been suffering from cluster migraines lately, and she was certain it was from her stressful encounters with Malachi. She gave Dreux half a smile and sighed.

"Better. My doctor put me on some stronger migraine pills, and hopefully, they work. My headache was so bad last night baby that I had to pull over onto the side of the road. I was scared I might crash, and you know that made me think of my wreck."

Dreux shook his head with his brows furrowed.

"Until we get this shit in order, I can take you wherever you need to go or get you a driver. You had me scared as fuck last night. I almost crashed trying to get to you. You know I can't handle nothing happening to you baby," he replied.

Billie nodded. She believed him because she felt the same way. Some may have felt it wasn't healthy, but her life wasn't worth living without her son or Dreux in it. They honestly completed her.

"I know baby, and I'll be fine. What's your plans for today?" she asked.

Dreux removed his hand and licked his fingers before gazing over at her. The way his sorrel hued eyes peered over at Billie, it made her heart race.

"A lot. I found a new location for my latest warehouse. I need to get that in order then meet up with my brothers' lawyer to see what's going on with his early release. I gotta meet up with Malachi too. You know I stopped by to see my mom's the other day, right?"

Billie nodded. She lit up her pink and chrome vape pod and hit it twice before glancing over at Dreux.

"Yeah, how is she doing? I have to go see her baby."

Dreux frowned. He licked his lips as he stared at Billie.

"She's good but why the fuck Malachi mom have her co-sign for a loan then dip out on her. She was getting ready to pay on it when I popped up at her house. The shit is for $40,000 and shit."

Billie's eyes widened. She scratched her scalp that was in dire need of a deep conditioning and shook her head. Let Malachi tell it he was paying the bills at his mother's home.

"What do you mean? So, she's losing the house?" she asked wondering what that meant for Malachi and her son.

"Nah, she's not cause my mom saved her lazy ass then she basically said fuck my mom. For some reason, my mom keeps letting my auntie shit on her. I'm not her though. I paid the loan off cause my mom not ever gone take the L, but I'm not either. I hit my auntie up twice and her ass trying to cry that broke shit, so I hit up her son. I told that nigga to hit me with $3,000, today or it was gone be a fucking problem, and I wanted $1500 a month from them. I'm not fucking around either. They paying me that shit back," Dreux said adamantly.

Billie sighed. $3000. Immediately she knew what her money was going to be put towards. Her insides coiled with anger as she thought of how fucking shady Malachi was.

"Wow I don't know what to say," she said quietly trying to mask her anger.

Dreux chuckled darkly as he sat up in the large bed.

"You ain't gotta say shit. I'm meeting up with that nigga at five, and he better have my shit or else. I wouldn't shoot him, but I would beat his ass. He not broke and neither is his cheap wine drinking ass mama," Dreux vented, and Billie had to smile.

Malachi's mom did love her some cheap ass wine.

"Well hopefully he will give it to you," she muttered knowing that he would because she was giving Malachi the money.

"Oh, he will. What you doing today?"

Billie thought of her upcoming errands as she hit her vape again. The smoke flowed through her nose as she stared at Dreux.

"Going to see my mom then the lawyer. You know court is coming up."

173

Dreux leaned towards Billie and ran his hands through her mass of ashe blonde strands. She closed her eyes as he massaged her scalp.

"I know, and you gone be good. Don't stress about shit baby. You want me to go see your mom with you?" he asked.

Billie's eyes peered open at her man. She wasn't sure what she'd done right in life, but damn she was lucky to have him.

"I thought you had plans today."

Dreux's thick brows pulled together. He licked his full lips as he stared at her intently.

"For you, I would cancel all that shit. Just say the word."

Billie's heart warmed at his words. She leaned in and sensually kissed his soft lips. Dreux gripped her strands, and she giggled against his lips.

"I love you, baby. How much you love me?"

Dreux chuckled still holding her strands hostage. He kissed her again, and his eyes ate her alive. Love, adoration, devotion, and loyalty sat in his lids as he peered at her.

"More than I ever loved anything in this fucking world sexy. That much. Come hop on this dick before you go," he told her and pulled a giggling Billie onto his lap.

An hour later Billie pulled up to the gas station near Malachi's job. She threw her car in park and grabbed her phone. After sexing Dreux she was ready to go back to sleep, but her day was just beginning. Her fingers moved swiftly as she sent off a text.

I'm here.

The message was immediately read with no response. Billie tapped her coffin natural colored nail on the middle console as she stared out of her car's window. Her body grew tired with every minute that passed. Her eyes grew heavy and as twenty minutes rolled around Malachi was tapping on her window. A cocky smirk sat on his chunky face as he stared down into the car. Like always he was rocking a fresh haircut with nice threads. He looked as if he was ready to hit the streets instead of hitting up his job.

Billie sucked her teeth as she looked him over.

She grabbed the neatly stacked money. Money that she'd busted her ass for. Money that she was hoping to put into her son's account, and she rolled her window down. She stuck her hand out and rolled her eyes.

She absolutely hated Malachi.

"Here's ten. I'll help you pay off the rest. Why would you tell me you were helping your mom when clearly you weren't?"

Malachi snatched the money from Billie's hand and placed it in his jean pocket. He leaned into the car and the strong stench of marijuana assaulted Billie's nostrils.

"Look, I was fucking helping her! She was taking my shit and not paying her bills. It's hard-taking care of a fucking kid when you doing the shit by yourself."

Billie's head snapped back, and she laughed lightly.

"You got some fucking nerve. Now you doing this by yourself? Yes, I fucked up. Yes, I messed up very badly, but I never once stopped providing for my child!"

Malachi nodded. He glared down at Billie as she frowned back at him.

"How the fuck you know about my family's business? You and that nigga must still be real close," he said referring to Dreux.

"Did I ever say we wasn't? I've been close with him since I was a damn teenager. That's how I know you! Don't start with me, Malachi. I can't believe you lied to me about getting your car fixed," she replied.

Malachi waved her off, and his shiny watch caught her eye.

"And I can't believe you dropped the ball and almost killed our damn son. Neither one of us is perfect. I hope you know he got a bitch. I heard she live with him too while you running behind him and shit. Looking dumb as fuck. You need to be focusing on being a good mom to Kawan and trying to make our family work," he told her.

Billie's eyes rolled as she stared straight ahead.

"Malachi you and I will never be nothing more than two people that made a child together. You need to focus on fixing what your mom did. That wasn't right," Billie said angered by his words.

"What!" Malachi moved quickly to pulled Billie's door open.

Billie tossed her car in drive and sped away as he hollered obscenities at her vehicle. Billie's heartbeat didn't slow down until she was pulling onto the freeway. Billie road to see her mother in silence. She was thankful for all of the things the Lord had blessed her with still an emptiness filled her insides when it came to her parents and her son. Her father was in another state playing house with his mistress while her mother suffered alone.

Billie had grown up in a nice upper-middle-class family. Had everything that a kid could want and while she modeled and lived out her dreams her parents secretly battled it out. Her father was a womanizer and to cope with his infidelities her mother turned to the casino. Her mom started a serious gambling addiction that resulted in them losing nearly everything.

178

After driving for forty-five minutes, Billie pulled up to the recovery center. Billie made good money modeling, and her income went to her son and her mom. To take care of them, she was close to being broke. Being the sole provider wasn't easy at all. And the truth was without Dreux, Billie wouldn't be living as comfortable as she was.

"Lord, let her be doing good today," she prayed before exiting her car.

Billie quickly went into the large white building and signed in. She was then checked for drugs and weapons before being sent through. Billie waited for twenty minutes before she was called to the visitation room. Her face lit up when she spotted her tall, modelesque mother at a white round table.

"Bethany! Look at you!" her mother Eva spoke excitedly.

Billie sighed with relief after seeing her mother's pleasant disposition. She rushed into her mother's slender arms and hugged her tight. Tears threatened to fall as Eva embraced her.

"I love you, pretty girl. You know that?" her mom whispered.

Billie nodded. She believed it. When they lost the house.

She believed it.

When they lost the cars.

She believed it.

When her mom cleaned out all the accounts including her modeling account that she'd had from the age of three...

She believed it.

Billie loved her mom and regardless of the things she done she knew in her heart that her mother loved her as well.

However, her mom had an addiction. Billie believed it was how she'd easily picked up her habit of drinking.

"I know ma, and I love you too."

They both sat down, and Billie's mother smiled at her. Billie matched the smile as she soaked in her mom's natural beauty. It was who she'd gotten her looks from. Eva was tall with striking features.

The perfect sized nose and lips. High cheekbones with slanted almond shaped eyes. Long thick ashe blonde hair and a slim frame. Eva was an investment banker before her fall. Had gone to school for it and was great at what she did.

"How are you doing?" Billie asked breaking the silence.

Eva shrugged.

"Okay, I guess. Some days are good, and some are really bad. It's my third time coming here, baby. I can't keep taking your money for this place and relapsing. I have to fix this addiction. I can't let it ruin any more of my good years. I wish I was as strong as you," her mom revealed.

Billie grabbed her mothers' soft hands and squeezed them gently.

"You are. God is faithful mommy. You taught me that, and he will get us through this. Don't worry about the money. Just take your time getting better."

Eva sighed with worry on her pretty caramel colored face.

"This place is $5,000 a month, Billie. You have Kawan and yourself to think of. Like I haven't done enough now you have to pay for this and its embarrassing. I feel like a failure," her mom revealed.

Billie let her mothers' hands go, and she stood up. She sat beside her mom and pulled her to her side. The money she didn't care about. You couldn't take the shit with you when you left the earth anyway. For the people she loved, she would do anything for them. That wasn't up for debate.

"Close your eyes mom," she instructed quietly.

Eva began to quietly weep as Billie held her.

"No weapon formed against us shall prosper. The God we serve is a mighty God. I pray in the name of Jesus that he delivers you from this addiction like he delivered me. Like he is still delivering me. I pray that he heals your pain, binds your wounds, and set you free. For he is the only one who can give you real joy. Real inner peace. Amen."

"Amen," Eva sniffled out.

Billie sighed. She rocked her mother back and forth slowly as she began to sing.

"Jesus loves me this I know. For the bible tells me so," she sung lowly.

Eva smiled with wet eyes as she joined in with Billie. It was a song that Billie's mother had often sung to her as a child.

"Yes, Jesus loves me. Yes, Jesus loves me," Eva sung out loud.

Billie exhaled as her body relaxed. Slowly her worry dissipated, and she knew in that moment that God was surrounding them. Billie kissed her mother's forehead as her own eyes misted over.

"We'll be fine. This too shall pass mommy," she whispered believing that it would.

What good was it to pray and worry? Billie knew that in order for the Lord to work you had to give all of your problems to Him.

Billie returned home late into the night tired. Her feet moved slowly as she walked through her bricked home. Trey Songs played from the upstairs garnering her attention. Billie stepped out of her heels and headed to the second floor.

Rose petals lined the hardwood floors and led to the bedroom. Billie's beautiful face stretched into a smile as she entered the master bedroom.

Their master bedroom.

"Dreux Kawan Jones. What are you up to?" Billie asked peering around her large bedroom.

A year ago, Dreux asked her to move in with him. Billie had been shacking up with Novah and hadn't planned on leaving anytime soon, but his request was well received. Billie accepted it and didn't regret it. Dreux owned a beautiful townhome in Midtown. The property was in an excellent location, and Billie knew that when he was ready to sell it, people would be fighting for the place.

"Trying to keep you smiling. I know it's always hard when you go see your mom. Take off your clothes," Dreux replied sitting in the large winged back chair that sat in the corner of their room.

Next to the nightstand beside the chair was a bottle of Roi Merde Rose. It was top notch liquor from Detroit's own rapper Kasam. And like Diddy when he brought out Cîroc or Rick Ross with his Bellaire, the drink was instantly a hit selling out in all of the stores.

Billie eyed the tall equiangular brown shiny bottle before looking at her man. Dreux sat slouched in the chair with a large black towel wrapped around his waist. His lusty hooded eyes deliberately ghosted up and down her slim body, and he licked his lips. His taper possessed a longer curly look to it; still, he donned a fresh line up. A smirk ghosted across his face as he stared her way. "Get naked and come here," he instructed.

Billie moved as if she were in a marathon stripping away her attire for the day. Once she was down to her birthday suit, she sauntered over to her man. Dreux pulled Billie onto his lap, and his erection attempted to break through the thick towel in search of her warm tunnel.

Dreux chuckled as he leaned towards her.

"That nigga looking for you like where she at? Where she at?" he joked.

Billie smiled. She laughed lightly until Dreux was removing the towel from his waist. He lifted Billie up and slid his member deep inside of her. Billie's body quaked with pleasure as she slowly slid down his thick dick. Dreux slapped her ass gently as he gazed up into her eyes.

"Damn, she wet and ready too. Bounce on it for me," he demanded.

Billie rode him faster as he cupped her 34 C cups. Billie's eyes rolled as her body grew warm. Already his thick ass dick was knocking against her spot. Billie's chest heaved up and down as she stared into Dreux's eyes.

"I love you so much baby," she whispered.

Dreux nodded. He tweaked her nipples as his teeth sunk into his bottom lip.

"I love the shit out of you too. Stick out your tongue," he commanded.

Like his love slave, Billie stuck out her pretty pink tongue. Dreux sucked on her tongue vigorously as he fucked her from the bottom. His large hands cupped her ass as he pulled Billie close to him. Billie's cries of pleasure came out muffled as her sex secreted love juices all over his member.

"Damn, this pussy so good," Dreux muttered.

He leaned Billie back and with her sitting on his lap with her head hanging back he fucked the shit out of her until they were both erupting so loudly, so strong that they broke the chair.

Two days later Billie watched her man as pride coursed through her veins. She cheesed a big stupid grin as he stood before the young impressionable men that were all in some local gang doing God knows what.

Dreux removed the Mitchell and Ness Detroit snap back, and his eyes peered intently at the group of young men. Briefly, he looked Billie's way, and she winked at him.

"I'll keep this quick. My man's runs this place and asked me if I could come through. I met him when we was around y'all age. We hung in the hood daily. Bragged bout things we didn't have and got into a lot of trouble. We both could have been dead or in jail, but we chose a different route. We saw how people was dying daily. We saw shit that I knew I didn't want for myself and I'm glad he felt that same way. We started back going to class. Pulled our grades up and we was both given scholarships. Going away to college was hard. I had to leave my family and the love of my life," he noted, and Billie swallowed hard when he looked at her.

Back then times was hard for them. She was always busy, and so was he. Life was pulling them in separate directions, and it was in those weak moments that she'd started to lean on Malachi. Malachi could never replace Dreux, but he had been a shoulder to cry on.

"I did what I had to do however to secure my future. My mom told me a long time ago that all I had was my education. Do you know what society thinks about young black men like yourselves?" he asked.

A few boys nodded while most stared blankly at Dreux. Dreux smirked at them before shaking his head.

"That if you want to hide something from black people, put it in a book. They don't expect y'all to live past 18. Shit now maybe 16 with the way the cops taking us out. I know better than anybody how it is growing up in Detroit. It's hard, but the only way you can change your life is to change yourself. Nothing happens by chance. I now own my own business. I got cars, money in the bank and property. That happened by hard work and dedication. I didn't steal to get it or sell drugs. I didn't have to, and I believe that if you are a hustler, you can hustle anything. I brought checks with me. I wanna help y'all beat the odds. Not be a statistic, but you gotta want that too. I'm giving away cash for scholarships but only to the people that want it," Dreux said, and Billie clapped before everyone else in the room.

Dreux's mother stood at her side clapping loudly as well. Both women calmed down once Dreux wasn't in front of the room, and Billie turned to his mother. They were close and always had been. Billie loved and respected her and often went to her with her daily issues.

"How are things going with you and my son?" his mom asked while smiling.

Billie watched Dreux speak with a couple of young black men, and she sighed. Things with him were....

Perfect.

"Great. I can't complain. How are you?"

Dreux's mother shrugged while staring Billie's way. She smiled, but it didn't quite reach her eyes.

"I've seen better days. It's a lot going on with the family right now. I'm not sure if he told you."

Billie's brows knitted together. She scooted closer to Dreux's mom, and she continued.

"I can't go into detail just yet, but I need for you to promise me something baby. Can you please hold off on telling everyone about you and my son? I need to fix things with everyone then you can tell them," his mom explained.

Billie stared at Dreux's mother intently. She wasn't rushing to tell Malachi about her relationship with his cousin anyway, but she knew her man. He was getting antsy. Tired of the shit being a secret. Billie feared that holding off Dreux would only cause more issues with her own relationship.

"But Dreux- "

"Needs to wait. Please," his mom begged quietly with worried lenses.

Billie quickly nodded hating the sadness that covered his mother's face. She rubbed her arm and smiled at her.

"I'll find a way to convince him we need to wait," she assured her.

Dreux's mother sighed and patted Billie's arm.

"Thank you so much sweetie," she replied as Dreux walked

over.

Billie's eyes skated up to Dreux, and she smiled as his mother stood up. He embraced his mom and spoke with her as Billie pondered over his mother's request. Billie was already keeping so much from Dreux. She was now asked to manipulate his mind to keep their love an even longer secret and that didn't sit well with her. Dreux was everything she ever wanted in a man, and Billie was certain that if she didn't let him know about everything that was going on soon it just might be enough to push him away.

6

#fomo

"What's this?"

Normani smiled sheepishly as she placed the printed-up logo and business papers in front of Tru. He sat at the island in their kitchen with a plate full of fresh fruit. Dior Sauvage clung to his burly frame as he peered up at Normani. His downturned eyes gazed at her intently, and he smiled.

"I see the papers and the logo. I asked you what it was?"

Normani swallowed hard. The last month had been hard as hell for her. She'd been forced to cut down her mommy time to attend school. Normani honestly didn't like it, but she was pushing through. However, while in school she saw her vision come to life. Hooking up with her old high school friend had been a blessing.

Together they'd created the perfect program for parents, and she was excited at getting it out there.

Now she needed...... money.

Contrary to what people believed it took more than a vision to build your dream. It took capital and to get her business off the ground she needed at least $50,000. Money, she had but didn't have because Tru only allowed for her to be on the checking account that never had more than $10,000 in it.

Normani blew that in a day or two. She'd been saving, but it still wasn't enough because she'd used most of her savings on school and daycare expenses for River.

"It's my new business. I applied for the name and handled everything on that end now I need money," she said quietly.

Tru stopped staring at Normani to look down at the papers. His brows drew together as he read over her business plan. He smiled at the logo before grabbing a piece of cantaloupe.

"Where River at and what I say bout them damn glasses? They big as shit ma. You need to burn them, bitches," he replied.

Normani groaned. She looked down at the papers in front of Tru and cleared her throat.

"She's with your mom, and I lost my contacts. I'm at home Tru. I can wear these damn glasses whenever I like."

Tru nodded slowly. He sat back and peered up at Normani. Like always her stomach fluttered at the sight of him. Even with all his bad ways he still did something to her. In his simple get up of a white beater with black jeans he looked sexy. He licked his thick lips, and she eyed the tattoo of River's name that went down the side of his left brow in small cursive writing.

"You can, but I thought we was in this shit together. The same way you like to shop, I make sure you can. The same way you like for a nigga to lick on that pussy, I make sure I do it just right. All I asked was for you not to wear some fucking glasses, and it's a problem? Huh?" he asked and slapped her ass.

Normani rolled her eyes, and he pulled her close to him. He bit her nipples through her top, and she moaned lightly.

"Do as daddy asked baby," he murmured before letting her go.

Normani slowly took off her glasses and with blurry vision stared at Tru. She watched him stare down at the papers again and shake his head.

"First school, now this. And River the one suffering. I ain't seen my baby girl in days. This shit is crazy. I thought you was focusing on our family. What happened to that?" he asked.

"Nothing but this is also important to me. You're living out your dreams. I want to do that as well. This is making me happy. Now I need the funds for it," she responded squinting her eyes to see where she put her phone at.

Tru nodded. He ate a few more pieces of fruit before standing up. He tugged at his sagging Balmain jeans as he looked at Normani.

"I'll see what I got in the accounts. I had to pay some bills and handle some other shit. I don't hit you with my problems cause

I don't want you to worry, but I'm in the middle of some legal shit right now."

Normani frowned at his words. He was saying everything but the right fucking thing.

"Legal like what? What's going on Tru and I know you have $50,000. Stop playing with me."

"I said I'll let you know! We been vibing good baby. No arguing and no fighting. Don't start acting up cause you not getting your way. A nigga can't always fucking say yes to you. I'll let you know in a few days," he replied.

Normani's face screwed up tight with anger. She turned and briskly walked off. Tru caught her as she was heading up the stairs and grabbed her arm. He hugged her from the back as his lips pressed against her soft neck that smelled of Mui Mui perfume.

"I'll get it for you when I can. I don't wanna fight ma. Get dressed and ride out with me. We'll grab River later on," he whispered before letting her go.

Normani angrily walked off. She rushed up the stairs and stepped into her bedroom. All week she'd been anticipating Tru saying yes and giving her the money. They weren't lacking for anything and the story of them suddenly being strapped for cash wasn't believable to her.

"Stop pouting and get dressed. Maybe put on that blue romper I like ma. None of that weird Solange looking shit you like to rock," Tru said stepping into the room.

Normani rolled her eyes as she walked towards her bathroom. She washed her hands and quickly put in her contacts. As her vision became clear again, she sighed. She wasn't blind without her glasses, but her life was much better with her glasses or contacts on. She then went over to her closet. She grabbed the first outfit she came across which happened to be the navy bell sleeved romper that Tru loved so much and she pulled it off the hanger.

Normani quickly changed her clothes and slid on a pair of gold YSL heels. As Normani put on a light face of makeup, Tru stepped into the bathroom's doorway. He peered at her intently as she applied her navy colored liquid lipstick.

"I love you. From the minute I saw you inside of the club I knew you would be mine. What's funny is that a nigga didn't have shit back then. All my shit was on lease even my fucking car, but you held me down. Left school to tour with me and helped me get us to where we at now. I appreciate you, and I love you for that. I know that nobody is gone love me like you do. Shit that nobody loves me like you, not even my money hungry ass momma."

Normani ignored his words and finished fixing her face. She fluffed her wand curls that had been applied to her onyx-hued hair, and she stared at herself in the mirror. She looked beautiful, and she was blessed, but her happiness with Tru was fading. With each disappointment from him, the love changed.

At one point in time, she felt like he could do no wrong. He was perfect to her, and maybe that was where she went wrong. Placing him on a pedestal that he quickly fell from. Tru had never been caught cheating, but Normani had her doubts. She just knew that her man was slick enough not to get caught. He knew she was bat shit crazy and if anything, ever surfaced about his cheating ways she'd gut his ass like a fish.

"You ready?" she asked turning to him.

Tru stood up off the door and adjusted his chain. He'd put on a collard designer tee and his sneakers for the day. Sexiness oozed off him and Normani. Together they made a striking pair and the way his eyes devoured Normani in her outfit told her that he approved of her look.

Tru especially loved when she wore high heels.

"Yeah, come here."

Normani frowned. Now wasn't the time to play roles. She was mad, and he would know it.

"No, let's go and get whatever you have to do over with so we can get our daughter. Since you so fucking perturbed about her being gone," she replied.

Normani walked towards the door, and Tru pulled her into his arms. He hugged her body tightly as her arms rested at her sides. Her eyes rolled to the back of her head as he cupped her ass.

"We a family and I'll do whatever for us to stay together. I know I'm not perfect, but for you, I can be," he told her.

200

Normani moved from his arms and nodded. His words were flowing through one ear and leaving out the other.

"So, you say," she murmured leaving him standing in the bathroom.

Quietly they exited the two-level home and got into Tru's latest toy a burnt orange R8. Normani detested the loud ass colored he had painted on the car but loved the car itself. She rode beside Tru lost in her thoughts. Like always his two cellphones fought for attention. Ringing back to back as he played his latest mixtape that he'd produced. Normally Normani would be all in hyping up her man but it was hard to be happy for him and his success when he hadn't asked her once about school or shown any interest in her business, she was attempting to get off the ground.

"How you like it so far? Is that Trill track hard?" he asked turning the music down.

Normani nodded still staring out of the window. She thought of Azariah. It had been a few days since she'd seen him and was already missing his handsome face.

201

"It's straight," she murmured.

Tru sucked his teeth. He turned the music back up, and twenty minutes later they were arriving at Detroit's latest happening restaurant Mon Amour. The owner happened to be in the building along with his brother, the platinum-selling rapper by the name of Draye. Tru had worked with him various times over the last five years and was close with him.

Normani exited from the car and smiled when she noticed a few paparazzi people snapping photos.

"Wow, Draco's crazy ass brought the paparazzi to the city tonight," she noted.

Tru grabbed Normani's hand and possessively pulled her to his side. He kissed her cheek lovingly, and a few more cameras went off.

"Yeah, it's a big party for his brother's latest album. His lil ass done broke all kind of records with his newest shit," Tru added and pulled them away.

Normani was happy that she was the kind of person that overdressed wherever she went because she fit right in with the crowd inside of the retro-urban chic five-star restaurant.

Inside the décor was black and white. Pop art large colorful photos covered the walls of the most notable hip-hop icons. Normani waved to a few people she knew in the industry thanks to Tru and her sister Novah. Tru led Normani over to a group of men all flanked in relaxed designer threads, and Normani immediately noticed them. It was Detroit's own Luca Gang along with the owner of the restaurant Draco and his beautiful wife Hill.

"Look at this nigga late like always and shit," Draco mused while chuckling.

Tru chuckled as he dapped up Draco.

"Whatever, this my lady Normani. Y'all know her sister Novah. She used to be real big in the video scene and shit," he said.

Everyone nodded and spoke to Normani. Hill gave her a quick hug and looked her up and down.

"I love that outfit. You too fine to be with him," Hill joked.

Normani smiled as Tru shook his head.

"I know, I was thinking the same thing about you," Normani replied, and everyone howled with laughter.

"Oh, I see why she with your ass. She quick on her toes," Draco said as Durand, one of the members of the Luca Gang stared down at Normani.

"Is your sis here?" he asked making everyone peer his way.

Draco smirked and ran his hand over his cleanly shaven head.

"Nigga, you can talk? I never heard your ass speak before. I thought you was the Tito of the group. Just around for a check and shit," he joked.

Durand smirked and waved Draco off.

"Whatever nigga but is she here?" he asked Normani again.

Normani stared up at the handsome rapper and slowly shook her head.

"She isn't, but I'll make sure to let her know you looking for her," she replied.

Durand's brows pulled together at her words.

"Nah, you ain't gotta do all that ma," he said before walking away.

"Damn, she got that nigga in his feelings," Draco chuckled.

A few people laughed, and Normani found herself staring across the room at a beautiful, tall thickly built woman. The woman wore a look of anger on her pretty round face as she stared Normani's way.

"You know her?" Normani whispered pulling on Tru's hand.

Tru glanced across the room, and his stance never changed. He shrugged before looking back to Draco.

"Girl these groupies do the most. Ignore her," Hill told Normani, and Normani shook the woman off.

Still, in the back of her mind, she made a mental note of how the girl looked.

205

Hours later the windows fogged up as Normani slid up and down Tru's hard dick. His large hands cupped her bare ass as he stared up into her eyes. After drinking for the last few hours and toking back a blunt they were both like dogs in heat. They couldn't get enough of each other.

"Tell me you never leaving me," Tru demanded pumping into her aggressively from the bottom.

Normani held onto Tru tightly as her snug walls hugged his member. Her eyes slid down into his, and for the first time ever she found herself stuck. Passionate as it was it still wasn't enough for her to lie. All night she'd watched her man in action. Smiled on his arm, interacted with people she gave no fucks about while he lived out his dream. It stung to realize that she'd always placed him first and he couldn't do the same for her.

Smack!

"Tell me, baby," he groaned and bit her neck.

Normani moaned. Her eyes closed and she gave way to the orgasm taking over her body.

206

"I.... I won't," she lied softly.

Tru grunted, and within seconds her body vibrated for him. A deep moan erupted from her and Tru grabbed the back of her neck. He pulled her face to his and stared into her eyes.

"Give me another baby," he demanded lustfully before shoving his soft tongue deep into her awaiting mouth.

Stacks of cash lined the maple desk. Behind the large desk sat the man that wouldn't leave her mind. Normani slowly sat down as she eyed him in his element. Azariah was an investment banker. He worked for his cousin's Qwote and Quamir at their finance company and was making big money for him to only be twenty-one. He was living out his dream. Doing things that he told her he would, and he was also helping her build her dream up.

Normani smiled at him as she grabbed the money. In his brown three-piece custom suit, he looked daddyish as hell. His fresh haircut and handsome smirk had her wanting to kiss him.

"Thank you," she murmured.

Azariah waved her off like giving her fifty thousand was nothing for him.

"Just make sure my homegirl knows who had her back in the end," he said referring to Normani's daughter River.

Normani smiled. She put the cash inside of her Hermes bag, a new gift from Tru and sat back in her seat.

"I promise I will. What have you been up to stranger?"

Azariah adjusted his tie as he peered her way.

"Working. I'm trying to reach a certain money goal this year, so I been grinding it out. I wanna be a millionaire before we hit twenty-five," he replied.

Normani nodded knowing that he could do it.

"I believe in you. I know you can do it," she said as the doors opened.

Normani glanced back and was shocked to see a pretty, tall, chocolate beauty strutting into the office. In her hand was a large food bag. She offered Normani a big smile as she moved past her.

"Your receptionist said I could come in. Am I interrupting something?" she asked setting the food on Azariah's desk.

Normani swallowed hard as she assessed the beauty. She was taller than her and had a lot more ass, but that's where the shit stopped for her. The woman's face was average as hell, and she had in a lace front that was kissing her brows. Normani hated when women wore unnatural looking wigs. She felt the weave field was far too advanced for women to be doing that petty bullshit.

"Nah, you good. This shit right on time. Thank you," Azariah said and stood up. He walked around his desk and pulled the woman into his arms. He kissed her passionately for several minutes before letting her go. "Aye, baby this my best friend Normani. The one I told you about," he said, and it was then that Normani was hit with the familiar perfume scent.

"Dollar Tree," she murmured looking up at the pair.

Dominique Thomas

Azariah held back his grin while the woman in his arms

frowned.

"I'm sorry, what?" she asked.

Normani shook her head.

"Nothing. It's nice to meet you."

Azariah shook his head as he let the woman go.

"Normani this Camilla. I met her when I was in school in

DC," he said taking his seat.

Camilla walked over to Normani and shook her hand. She

took a step back, and Normani was again assaulted with the tacky

scent of her perfume.

"Hi, well I should get going. I'll meet you at your place later

baby, and it was nice to meet you Normani," Camilla said.

Normani nodded not bothering to respond, and Camilla

smiled. She doubled back and gave Azariah another kiss before

exiting the office. As Azariah pulled food from the brown bag,

Normani glared at him.

"Ugh! She's ugly as hell, and she wears cheap perfume. Really Azariah?"

Azariah chuckled.

"Tru is ugly and a dog ass nigga to you. Really Normani?" he mimicked her.

Normani pouted while folding her arms. She rolled her eyes, and Azariah sat back in his seat.

"What the fuck do you want from me? You said friendship, so that's what a nigga giving you. Now when you ready for more let me know. I can't sit around with a hard dick and no woman. That's fair to me? What the fuck," he grumbled.

Normani sighed. She watched him tear into his steak salad as her heart grew heavy.

"Whatever. Thanks again for the money. I promise to pay you back."

Azariah watched her stand. He took a few bites from his food before standing up. When he walked up on her Normani swallowed hard.

211

"I'm not gone beg you to be with me, ma. I'll take you, however, I can to have you in my life but as long as you with that nigga I'ma do me. You still my favorite girl though and you know that shit. Come here," he said and pulled her into his arms.

Normani hugged Azariah tightly before leaving his office. Normani grabbed her daughter from daycare before heading home. Azariah and his tacky broad plagued her mind as she pulled into her driveway. When she spotted Tru's newest toy a white two-door foreign car, she sighed.

"I thought his ass was going out of town," she mumbled not in the mood to see him.

Normani grabbed her things and got her daughter out of her car before heading into her home. Rose petals greeted her at the door along with soft R&B music. Normani's face lit up as she stepped through the door.

"Tru! What's going on!"

"Dada-dada!" River yelled while wiping her eyes.

Normani smiled at her baby girl.

"There go my two favorite girls. Come here," Tru said walking towards Normani.

In his hand was a small Louie carryall. Normani's carry all to be exact. Normani sat her daughter down and watched her baby girl charge towards her father at lightning speed. Normani soaked in the romantic ambiance of the room and sighed.

"What's going on Tru?" she asked again.

Quieter this time.

Tru sat the luggage down and picked up River. He kissed her cheek before stalking over to Normani. His intoxicating scent made it to Normani before he did and once, he reached her he planted a wet, soft kiss to her heart-shaped lips.

"Us, that's what's happening," Tru replied and dropped down to one knee.

Normani's mouth fell open as she watched him pull a small red box from his left pocket. Tru looked nervous as he gazed up at her.

"For any pain, I ever put you through I'm sorry. It was never my intention to bring pain your way. I know I can be a lot, but I'm yours and you mine. I love the hell out of you Normani. You gave me something priceless and you the only woman I can ever see myself being with. I need you to marry me beautiful. Can you do that?" he asked sincerely.

Normani stared down at him in shock. He wore a black tux that fit him to a "T." Her favorite scent wafted over the space surrounding them. Instead of thinking about how he was she envisioned who he could be. She envisioned him being a better man to her. A better father to their daughter and her heart swelled with love. The fear of missing out on giving her daughter a legit family hit her. She wasn't brave enough to say no. Azariah was doing him, and she needed to do her. She needed to at least see if being Tru's wife was for her. Normani nodded slowly, and Tru grinned.

He opened the ring box and a stunning solstice diamond shined in the dimly lit hallway. He pulled the ring from the box as River slept peacefully on his right arm. That quick she'd gone back to sleep.

"Normani Marie Royale will you marry me?" he asked slowly.

Normani nodded while cheesing hard. She leaned down and allowed for Tru to place the stunning diamond onto her finger. He gazed up at her intently as his body relaxed.

"Tonight," he added in quietly.

Normani looked up from her ring and her eyes connected with his.

"What did you say, baby?"

Tru stood and licked his lips. He adjusted his daughter so that she would be more comfortable and cleared his throat.

"I want you to marry me tonight. I rented out a jet. It's waiting on us right now. Let's do it with just us," he said lowly.

Normani gazed up at him with her heart racing. She looked at her daughter and swallowed hard. This was what she'd been wanting. A real commitment out of him. They would now be an official family. A unit and then he'd listen to her. He'd value her needs as well, and she wanted nothing more than to make that happen.

She stepped closer to Tru and grabbed his hand. A big smile covered her pretty face as she nodded.

"Yes, let's do it. Let's get married tonight," she replied making him smile.

Relief flooded Tru's face as he stared up at her.

"You don't even know how happy you just made a nigga," Tru replied before giving her a kiss.

7

#backtoback

"What's going on in that pretty little head of her's? She up and do some shit like marriage without consulting me and that illiterate fool Tru! How dare he ask my daughter's hand in marriage without speaking to me about it! I can't believe them," her mom vented.

Novah's heart seemed to temporarily stop. She stared at the white plastic stick once more as she listened to her mom rant.

Pregnant.

How?

The fuck?

He'd worn condoms all that night. He'd ensured that she

not drink over the limit and she remembered it all. The passion.

The pleasure. His big ass dick. The orgasms—

"And she calls me once it's done like everything is all good. I

know no one is perfect, but Tru has a lot of things he needs to work

on before being my baby's husband. If only your father was still alive

none of this mess would be happening," her mom said, and Novah

was pulled into another emotion.

One of grief. She closed her eyes and prayed that she was

dreaming. None of this was real. Her sister hadn't just up and

married her sometimes good baby daddy, and she wasn't pregnant.

All was well, and she was just in a sick ass nightmare.

Novah opened her eyes when she heard her mom sniffle,

and she cleared her throat.

Nope, it was very much happening.

"Mom it's okay. I wish dad was still here too. I'm sure a lot

of things would be different had he still been alive. I need to get

ready for court. Can I call you back?"

"Yes, is my nephew coming with you?" her mom asked.

Novah thought of her cousin Arquez and smiled.

"Yes, he is. He's actually on his way right now. I'll let you know what happens when I leave."

"Okay baby and don't be worried. The Lord has already handled everything," her mom assured her before ending the call.

Novah put her cell away and stared down at the plastic stick. She looked up at the ceiling inside of her large bathroom and swallowed hard. She wasn't on birth control, but she didn't feel the need to be. She wasn't consistently having sex. Now that she was possibly pregnant, she regretted not being on at least the damn pill. She'd only taken the test because of her missed period.

"A baby, but how? I don't even know this fucking man. Another public figure. Another person I'm not married to. Hell, we're not even friends let alone in love, and I may be pregnant by him. This is un fucking real," she griped.

Novah forced herself to get up from the toilet. Her ass had gone numb anyway from sitting so long. As she rubbed her bottom, she looked at herself in the mirror. Her mocha skin shined under her light's vanity. She smiled wryly at herself and licked her lips. Her eyes slid down to her flat abdomen and uncertainty ran through her. She rubbed her belly as thoughts of being pregnant filled her mind.

"I can barely handle the twins I have. I don't need this right now God. I'm not ready for another kid," she said silently and walked away from the mirror.

Novah took a hot shower making sure not to get her bouncy curls wet. She then got dressed putting on a coral colored two-piece suit with a white blouse. On her feet was a pair of nude heels while gold jewelry decorated her neck and wrist. Novah ran her hands through her hair making her bouncy curls appear messy in a cute way, and she grabbed her clutch.

Her cellphone rung as she ascended the stairs. Novah rushed to open her door and standing on the other end was her cousin Arquez. He held a serious look to his handsome face as he stared down at her. Arquez looked nice in his white Fendi crew neck monster tee that he'd paired with dark jeans and Off-White sneakers. A Cuban diamond chain hung from his neck as a diamond watch adorned his wrist. Novah smacked her lips as she gazed up at him.

"Who told you to do all that? We not hitting up somebody's runway show. We just going to court," she joked.

Arquez chuckled. He waved her off as she locked up her home.

"I dress like this every damn day. Stop playing with me. You good?"

"I am," Novah lied wishing she was as they headed to Arquez's white Mercedes.

They slid into the sleek sedan, and as Arquez pulled off, Novah received a text from her sister. She pursed her lips as she opened the message thread.

You and mom is acting real funny style right now. I expected for my family to be happy for me. Not this but regardless of your pettiness, I wish you well. I pray you don't have to split custody with that fuck nigga. Keep me posted sis.

Novah sighed as she text her sister back.

221

I pray I don't either, and we are happy for you. We just don't appreciate how you did it. We would have liked to be included in your plans but whatever. If you're happy, then we are too. I'll call you when I leave.

"Normani?"

Novah nodded peering over at her cousin. The fact that he was taking time out of his hectic schedule to attend court with her meant a lot.

"Yeah. She's upset that me and mom is mad about the marriage. Well not really even the marriage. I hate that we had to wake up to news online that she'd been married. It's like why the rush?"

Arquez shook his head. He pulled onto the freeway and briefly glanced over at Novah.

"Normally I would keep my fucking mouth shut. I don't like to be interfering in people's business. That ain't never been my style but some shit with Palmer's people happened a while back, and it had me wondering if things could have played out differently had I spoke up? I could have at least told Palmer, but I didn't so I'ma lace you with this. Word on the street is that Tru got a kid. I never saw or met the bitch, but a few people I fuck with say its legit. That could be why he rushed and did that shit. I think they said the kid is only a few months old," Arquez replied.

Novah's heart fell to the pit of her stomach. Her sister could scream fuck Tru all night and day, but she loved him. Loved his dirty damn drawers and she knew Normani would be crushed if this rumor was in fact true.

"I don't know what to say," she mumbled shocked by her cousins' words.

Arquez shrugged while frowning.

"Tell her now and let her check into the shit. That's all you can do," he told her.

Novah nodded praying that the stories of Tru having a kid was just that, an exaggerated tale from people with too much time on their hands.

Thirty minutes into court Novah was ready to blow a gasket. Her narrowed eyes couldn't help but to glare over at her shady ass baby daddy. Carter sat in his seat wide-eyed and arrogant. The black two-piece suit fit him perfectly as he like always rocked his jewelry showing off his wealth. A wealth that he claimed was dwindling down.

Carter's lawyer stood in front of the judge with a manila folder. Novah's chest heaved up and down as she pondered over what they were up to.

"Your honor my client wants more time with his sons. Ms. Royale is denying him of that time while living a reckless life. I have photos date and stamped with Ms. Royale partying recklessly. Even a video of her engaging in public sexual activity while under the influence of alcohol," Carter's lawyer said loudly.

"What the fuck!" Novah yelled outraged.

Novah's head snapped Carter's way, and he winked at her. She looked to her lawyer, and her lawyer, a pretty brown skinned woman, stood abruptly.

"Your honor my client was asked to give the defendant more time because of his drug abuse. He was charged for dropping dirty, and that is why we are in court. How my client spends her time is irrelevant to this case," Liberty spoke up.

The judge looked from Novah's lawyer to Carter's handsome lawyer. She sighed as she took the folder.

"Let me check these out. The case is about a parenting agreement. Mr. Edmonds would like to split custody, and if Ms. Royale is using her time to party then I see no reason as to why he shouldn't be able to have more time with his children," she replied snidely.

Carter's low chuckle made Novah sink her teeth into her bottom lip.

"What video could they have of you?" Novah's lawyer asked sitting down.

Novah shrugged. She did nothing. Had no fucking life outside of her kids. Yes, she went to the bar every blue moon but not enough for Carter to have a valid case against her. He partied

way fucking harder than she did.

"These my people, relax. This not no industry shit. Is it?"

Durand's words came back to Novah full force as she stared

straight ahead. She remembered the fingering, the lust, the passion

she felt in the room, and her shoulders sagged. He swore they

would be fine, and she prayed that the video Carter had of her was

not that.

"I'll need a few minutes," the judge spoke before exiting the

room.

"Bet you wish you would have just taken my offer. Now your

ass might have to pay me child support," Carter hackled.

"Ignore him," Novah's lawyer advised lowly.

Novah glanced over at Carter and wondered just when did

he become so hateful? She shook her head wishing she could slap

the smile from his face, and he laughed.

"I mean this shit is fucking comical to me. You gone learn who you fucking with, ma. You know I play to win, with your hot ass pussy," he jested.

Carter's lawyer leaned over to whisper in his ear, and Novah's leg began to shake. Knots formed in her stomach as she leaned up to rest her elbows onto the table.

"What's the matter? You good? Looking a little sick over there," Carter laughed.

"That would be enough," the judge said entering back into the courtroom. She sat down and licked her thin lips. Her ocean blue eyes peered at Novah and Carter as she cleared her throat. "After reviewing the paperwork, I see no reason as to why Mr. Edmonds can't split custody with Ms. Royale. The new support order is as follows. From Thursday to Sunday the children, King and Karter Royale will be with Mr. Edmonds. From Sunday through Thursday the children will be with their mother, Novah Royale. The new child support order is $5,000 per child. Ms. Royale, I would watch my behavior when in social settings because it is important to behave in a good manner at all times," she said before standing up.

Everyone in the room stood with the judge, and Novah stared blankly ahead as the judge exited the courtroom. Carter laughed rambunctiously as Novah's lawyer turned to her.

"Aww man this shit is hilarious!" he cracked while laughing as hard as he could.

"We can appeal. Don't worry," Novah's lawyer told her.

Novah looked past her lawyer and over at Carter. He stood tall and handsome as he smiled back at her.

"Nigga went from paying $24,000 to $10,000. I'll be to get my boys on Thursday. You have a good day Novah. Maybe use your extra time to spend with that hoe ass nigga you was chilling with. A fucking rapper, like you, ain't getting enough money from me. I see your hoe ass still on the hunt and shit. Guess you'll be popping out his baby soon too. You know you bitches love to come upon a nigga real quick and shit," he spoke harshly.

Novah's feet moved with no permission. Within seconds she was running up on Carter. He smiled until her fist flew into his nose. The bailiff along with Novah's lawyer pulled her back.

"Novah, relax," Arquez said stepping into the room.

Carter held his bleeding nose as he looked from Novah to her cousin.

"Mam we'll have to take you in for that," the bailiff said pulling out his handcuffs.

Carter quickly shook his head. He wiped his nose that didn't seem to want to stop leaking.

"I'm not pressing charges. She's good," he said to the guard.

The bailiff shook his head.

"It's not up to you. I have to do this," the bailiff insisted.

Novah glared at Carter as she was being obtained. If looks could kill Carter would have died on the spot. The hatred in Novah's eyes was enough for him to take a step back.

"Why?" she snarled bitterly. "I didn't ask for any of this. I didn't ask for you to cheat on me. I didn't ask for you to be a hoe ass nigga. You did all of that on your own. You are making my life a living hell. I hate you! I fucking hate you Carter!" she screamed with tears flowing down her face.

229

Carter's eyes softened. He swallowed hard before quickly

exiting the room. Arquez stared him down, and once he was gone,

he walked over to his cousin.

"I'ma take care of you. Just relax cousin and don't fight with

these niggas in here."

Novah nodded. Sadness covered her frame as she was taken

away in handcuffs.

- - - - - - - → ♠ ←- - - - - - -

"I love you, and I want you to pick up every time I call.

Okay?"

Karter nodded while gazing at her while King did nothing.

He stood immobile inside of the foyer with his Avenger backpack

on. Novah kissed Karter's forehead and looked at King.

"I will call every hour to check on you—"

"This isn't necessary, and can I come in? I have to relieve

my bladder," Mrs. Peterson said walking up.

Novah stopped looking at her boys to cut her eyes at Carter's mom. All that nice shit was dead. Even after Carter played her, broke her heart, and ruined the trust they had, she gave him the benefit of the doubt. Played nice when she should have been raising hell and this was the thanks, she got for it. Novah was over being the good one.

"No, you can't. Right there on the steps is fine, or you can go back to your outdated ass car," she quipped rudely.

Mrs. Peterson's jaw fell slack. Her head snapped back, and her eyes grew wide. She smiled as she nodded.

"I get it. You're upset, but you have no right to be. He is an amazing father, and that's something you can't take away from him. The way you and those boys live is all because of my son. He has always paid his child support and has never let you or those kids go without. If you speak to me like that again I will be forced to tell him about it," she warned Novah.

Novah laughed lightly. She ran her small hand through her inky black wavy hair and sighed.

"So, he can do exactly what to me? I'm not his wife, and I'm done with the shits. Grace you will never be allowed inside of my home again. This house belongs to me and me alone. I had money before your son, and I'll have money when he's long gone. I'm only going to ask you once to back the hell up out of my doorway," Novah replied.

Mrs. Peterson's mouth tightened. She curtly nodded and backed out of the doorway. She held onto her purse tightly as she waited on the porch. Novah glared at her for a moment before looking to her boys. While Karter was on his tablet oblivious to the turmoil happening around him, King looked up at Novah intently.

The sadness in his eyes made Novah regret acting in such a way, but Carter and his family were difficult. They didn't appreciate her when she was being nice. They didn't respect her then so now she would demand that shit. If they weren't coming at her the right way, then they wouldn't be able to come at her at all.

Novah was done with the bullshit.

"Mommy loves you so much, baby. Me and your daddy both does. You two have fun," she told them.

Novah kissed her son's goodbye before leading them to the door. Mrs. Peterson looked at Novah and cleared her throat.

"Novah," she said quietly.

Novah shut the door in her face refusing to say anything else to the mean ass old lady. The second the door hit her back she slid down it. Minutes later her tears fell from her face.

I'm lookin' in the mirror

At this woman down and out

She's internally dyin'

I know this was not what love's about

I don't wanna be this woman

The second time around

Five hours later Novah gazed out onto her large backyard. Her first Thursday night without her twins had her vexed. Anger, sadness, and emptiness moved through her being. She hugged her body as she experienced a mild migraine.

First trimester woes were upon her. She'd taken four more tests before finally caving in and visiting her doctor's office. Novah was indeed with child and to receive that news right after learning

she now shared custody with Carter was another blow to her chest.

Back to back, she was receiving life-changing news.

She was still shocked at how she'd lost her case to Carter

over what she felt was privilege and biases. Carter was a well-known

NFL player that had won two championships. She was merely a

video model with two kids by him that didn't know when to stop

partying. Novah knew she was much more than that, but in the eyes

of social media, she knew that was all she was known for.

Her cell vibrated on the glass table making her eyes shift its

way. She watched her sister's name slide across the screen, and she

shook her head. Novah didn't want a shoulder to cry on. She didn't

even want a listening ear.

At the moment she only wanted to pretend it didn't happen.

Another call came into her phone, and her brows dipped.

Novah noticed the unknown facetime call, and her frown deepened.

If it was Carter calling her to rub it in her face, she was sure she was going back to jail. He'd been so afraid to see her earlier that he'd sent his ignorant mother to collect the twins.

"What!"

Novah answered frowning into the screen. The call connected and the handsome chocolate face that stared back at her wasn't Carter's or his wife's. No, it was the other person responsible for her anger.

Durand sat inside of his car with a small smirk on his handsome mug. Novah rolled her eyes, and he chuckled.

"Damn, what I do to you? You mad I got your number?"

Novah's eyes shifted back to her backyard as she swallowed hard.

"What do you want?" she asked lowly.

Durand breathed into the phone.

"Honestly?"

Novah nodded. Sadness was exhausting, and she was on the verge of falling out from being filled with it.

"Yes, I have a lot going on, and I'm not looking to play any games. Because of you, I lost full custody of my kids."

Durand frowned at her response.

"How? What the fuck are you talking about?" he asked with knitted brows.

Novah looked back at her screen and saw he was peering at her intently.

"I had court today for split custody of my kids. While in court my ex showed the judge a video of you fingering me. I believed you when you said that it wouldn't get out, but it did. I listened to you, and I got fucked in the end! Don't fucking call me again," she replied and ended the call.

Novah sat her phone down, and Durand called her back. For five minutes he attempted to video call her before calling her through audio. Novah snatched up the phone as more angry tears slid from her eyes.

"What?"

"Look, when I said it was all my people, I meant that shit. If what you saying is true, then I'll get to the bottom of it. I'm sorry that happened. Can I see you?"

Novah closed her eyes. Everything in her wanted to say no. She'd turned down her mother, sister and best friends visit, but Duran was different. He could offer her the kind of comfort that her body needed, but still, it didn't feel like it was the right thing to do.

"I don't know," she sighed with a sad tone.

Durand cleared his throat.

"I can't stop thinking about you. I apologize for all that shit that happened today. Even the shit I didn't have anything to do with. Let me ease your mind. Come on," he said nearly pleading in his deep voice.

Novah rolled her eyes hating how weak the body could be at times.

"Okay," she replied quietly. "I'll send you my address."

Novah ended the call and shared her location with Durand. She continued to sit on her patio until he was calling for her to open her front door. A million thoughts raced through her mind as she headed for the door. Novah wondered on if she would tell him of the baby but opted out of doing so. She wasn't ready yet. She could only deal with so much at one time.

"I'll tell him next time," she murmured unlocking her front door.

Novah pulled her large glass door open, and Durand stood on the other end. A black fitted cap sat low on his head. He wore a black crew neck t-shirt with black Nike basketball shorts. On his feet were a pair of Jordan's while a shiny Patek sat on his wrist. His scent flooded into the home as he stepped in.

Novah stared up at him nervously. She wore a black silk spaghetti strap nightgown that clung to her curvy frame. Her wavy locks were all over her head as her puffy eyes gazed Durand's way. He closed the door without speaking and pulled her into his arms.

Novah's body fell into his, and she sighed. Durand picked her up, and her legs went around his waist. He carried her up the stairs, and after looking twice through the rooms, he went into the master bedroom. Novah held him tightly as he took her over to the large canopy bed that sat in the middle of the room.

Durand sat down, and Novah pulled back to stare into his eyes. She had so many questions but no strength to ask them.

"You sure it was a video of us?" he asked.

Novah nodded, and Durand gritted his teeth. He removed his cap, and Novah was blessed with an up-close sight of his waved-up hair. She watched his jaw tense as he cleared his throat.

"I'll get to the bottom of that shit. I know it won't change anything, but I am sorry. I can only imagine how that made you look to the judge and shit. I'm sorry," he apologized and kissed Novah tenderly.

Novah closed her eyes as the word pregnant flashed through her mind.

"I'm real fucking sorry beautiful," he said kissing her neck.

His lips left a trail of passion on her skin. Durand gripped her bottom, and she moaned lightly. His large hands roamed up her back and under her nightgown. He pressed her closer to him as her breathing picked up.

"I missed you," he confessed lowly.

A small smile graced Novah's face as she looked at him.

He was ridiculously handsome. Slanted eyes with nice thick lips and the perfect straight nose. Definitely the full package.

"You don't even know me."

Durand smirked. He licked his lips and kissed her lips once more.

"And I'm ready for us to change that. Two months without seeing your pretty ass face really isn't fair. Let's be friends," he said and kissed her softly. Novah giggled, and he kissed her again. "Then lovers," Durand kissed her one more time, and his eyes peered into her intently. "Then something much more than that. Deal?"

Novah nodded falling into a spell he'd effortlessly placed on her. Durand grinned as he raised her nightgown over her head.

"I'ma make your body feel good, ma then when you get up in the morning we gone get to the bottom of some shit. Okay?"

Novah nodded again feeling relieved to have him there. It had been a while since she'd had a male take charge and assure her everything would be fine. For so long she'd been her own backbone. She didn't know how creditable Durand was, but for the moment she was giving him the benefit of the doubt.

"And we can't just go over it tonight?" she asked as the cool air kissed her bare skin.

Durand placed her on the bed naked and stood up. He quickly stripped out of his clothes and grabbed a Magnum XL from his Damier Ebene printed wallet. As he slid it on his massive hard-on, he gazed down at Novah.

"Nah, after this dick gets up in you, you gone be down for the count," he replied.

He said it in a matter of fact kind of way. Novah gulped and opened her thick thighs. Her fingers caressed her slick slit as she watched Durand hover over her.

"You been thinking bout me?"

Novah nodded as the pad of her finger rubbed in circular motions around her clitoris.

"I have," she admitted breathlessly.

Durand's teeth sunk into his bottom lip. He leaned towards Novah and her legs wrapped around his waist. As he inserted his thick head at her opening, he stared down into her eyes.

"This the last time we gone go months without seeing each other. I want you and not just your body. I want all of you," he declared, and with one swift motion, his member was deeply rooted in her sex.

Novah whimpered and closed her eyes. Durand attacked her lips aggressively as his dick fucked her in a way that only he could. In a way that Novah feared no one else could ever come close to doing.

"Talk to me sexy."

Novah licked her swollen lips. Durand loved to kiss, and she loved to kiss...... him. For hours, the night before she'd been his love slave. Her body had been his for the taking, and now she was dead ass tired. Her limbs weren't used to the twisting and pulling. Her pussy wasn't used to limitless pleasure. Her body wasn't used to back to back orgasms. She was drained; however this time it was in a good way.

As she rode beside Durand in his truck, she deliciously ached all over. Her attire for the day was chill. Cut up jean Bermuda shorts with a navy spaghetti strap bodysuit and leather slides. Oversized Chloe shades covered her eyes while her hair resided in a messy bun. She turned to Durand and marveled at how attractive he was. She wasn't the type to, but damn he was the shit.

He'd taken her back to his place so he could change and grab a bag of clothes. Dressed up or down he was handsome as hell. His chocolate skin bounced off his sexy frame. His fit for the day was designer track pants with the matching collared shirt. On his feet were black designer kicks while his fresh haircut screamed look at me. Novah found herself reaching over and rubbing his forearm that housed a scripture tattoo.

Durand glanced over at her as he pulled up to his studio that was located in Oak Park.

"You good?"

No, I'm having pregnancy migraines like a bitch.

"I'm fine, and it's a long story but here's the condensed version. Carter asked me a few months back to split custody with him. He claimed that he dropped dirty for coke at work and was placed on suspension. He said that he also had to pay a lot of money and that it was tight for him. I immediately called bullshit on that. Although he's flashy, he's good with his money. I didn't think he was anywhere near broke. I said no simply because his wife that was his mistress while he was with me doesn't like my sons. I felt like the time he did see them was enough. Carter didn't like that, and he showed his ass. Called me all kinds of names even kicked my truck with my boys in it. I brushed it off, and he served me with papers for court. My cousin Arquez was able to get me what he said was a good lawyer—"

"Quez? He cousins with Tarik?" Durand asked parking in his designated parking spot.

Novah nodded as she smiled.

"Yes, that Quez. I forgot he knows everybody, but court didn't go well Durand. They brought up pictures of the few times I did go to the bar, and somehow, they had a video of us. I wasn't able to view it, but the judge did, and I know that it influenced her decision. He now has split custody of our twins, and he only has to give me $5,000 per kid when I was only getting $12,000 before which wasn't a lot. I'm not trying to drain his bank account, but he makes a lot of money Durand. My kids should be able to have some of that, right?"

Durand pulled out his blunt and sparked it up. Novah rolled the window down hating the smell in her current state. She covered her nose, and Durand glanced over at her.

"You want me to put it out?" he asked.

Novah nodded avoiding eye contact with him, and he quickly did. He tossed the small blunt out the window and licked his lips.

"Every situation is different but what I can say is that every father should provide for their kid. I'll go without before my fucking kids do. For him to do all that bullshit tells me that he's a hoe ass nigga. I'm not feeling him even handling you like that. How long has he been like this?"

Novah removed her glasses and rubbed her eyes. She was still extremely tired.

Good dick had a way of doing that to you.

"Since I broke things off with him. Honestly, in the beginning, I would double back. If he wanted to slide through, then I was okay with that. I still loved him, but once he officially got with the bitch that's now his wife, I cut him off. I didn't play that side bitch shit, and after that, he was a different person. Some days he was nice, but whenever I shut off his advances, he acted a fool on me."

Durand nodded slowly.

"And he started disrespecting you?"

Novah sighed. She looked at Durand, and he caressed her cheek. The intent gaze he pushed her way made her emotional. No one really knew about Carter's disrespect. She always shielded it to keep the peace, but it felt good, to be honest.

"Yes."

"Has he ever hit you before?"

Novah quickly shook her head.

"No, but he has grabbed me inappropriately and forced me to kiss him. Done things like shoved his hands in my pants," she said quietly.

Durand leaned towards Novah and kissed her cheek.

"You don't deserve any of that baby. Remember that the next time he tries it, then you tell me when he does," he said lowly.

Novah's moist lenses connected with him.

247

"I don't want drama," she said with her stomach becoming queasy.

Durand nodded.

"And as long as he stays on some chill shit, I won't give him none. I'm not trying to make shit harder for you, but I can't sit back and let him wild out on you like that either. I get why you probably haven't told your people, but I wanna do more with you then make you cum. This shit is crazy, but I'm drawn to you ma. From the moment I met you at the spa you been on my mind. I feel protective over you already, and I'm not gonna let somebody hurt you. No matter who it is. You don't need your cousin to be your rock. I can be that for you. Let me."

Novah kissed Durand and pulled back to stare into his eyes.

"Why should I? I haven't met a man yet that can be good to me," she told him truthfully.

"I can't speak on them other niggas, but as for me I don't wanna do shit but make you happy. I'm far from perfect. I work a lot and travel more than I care for now that I'm older, but I'm a real ass nigga. I don't cheat, and I don't lie. With me what you see is what you get. The way I feel bout you did catch me off guard, but I'm not gone run from it. I'm a grown ass man. We vibing and we connecting. Let's embrace it, and while doing so, we gone be good to each other. I wanna be really fucking good to you Novah. Don't put what that hoe ass nigga did to you one me. Don't make me wear that hat, ma. Okay?"

Novah stared at Durand for a few minutes before nodding. She smiled, and Durand kissed her full lips before exiting his truck. They walked hand in hand into the studio. Marijuana smoke billowed out of the large room as Durand opened the door. Novah immediately covered her nose. She walked in, and all eyes turned their way.

"Nigga finally decided to show his face," Malano, Durand's group mate jested as he walked in.

"Right been hitting his ass all day and shit. I was close to putting out an Amber Alert on his ass," his other group mate Trill cracked while smirking at Durand.

Durand waved off his boys that he'd been friends with since childhood.

"Man fuck y'all niggas. Everybody this Novah," Durand spoke pulling Novah to his side.

Novah gazed up at him as her stomach lurched again.

"I'ma go to the bathroom and hi guys."

Durand stared down at Novah with furrowed brows. He leaned down and kissed her softly while gripping her waist.

"You good? You look sick."

Novah nodded. The watery bile coming up made her pull away from Durand and rush out of the room. She ran to the closest bathroom and as soon as she entered the empty stall the contents of her stomach spilled into the commode. Novah frowned as she spit up everything, she'd eaten that day. Her head ached ferociously as she stood up.

"Let's get you cleaned up," Durand said pulling her out of the stall.

Novah jumped and turned to him. Her hand flew to her chest as she looked up into his eyes.

"You scared the shit out of me," she said and laughed nervously.

Durand looked her up and down. He turned on the water and wet a paper towel for Novah. Novah stood still as he cleaned her face. He then tossed the towel and kissed her forehead.

"Come on," he said before pulling her away.

For two hours Novah sat inside of the studio with Durand and his group mates. She met Malano's wife Quinn and her best friend Erin who was Durand's old manager Kasam's, wife. Novah felt at home and welcomed amongst everyone, and that eased her nerves still she couldn't shake her stomach and headache woes. She rested on the leather sofa with her head propped up on Quinn's jacket as Durand wrapped up his verses on their new song.

"Hey this should make you feel better," Quinn said passing Novah some ginger pills along with a bottle of water.

Novah smiled as she took the items.

"Thank you so much."

Quinn shook her head. She was gorgeous in person, and Novah felt the pictures she'd seen of her online did her no justice.

"Girl we've all been there. Pregnancy is a bitch."

"Yes, it is," Erin added in as she sat beside Quinn.

Novah's heart raced at Quinn's words. She noticed Malano and Trill staring at her, and she felt herself getting light headed.

"I'm not pregnant girl," she laughed.

Quinn and Erin joined in with her as Durand stepped out of the booth.

"Oh, my bad. I'm not trying to put that nine-month sentence on you. Let's exchange numbers so we can hook up for lunch. Any friend of Durand's is a friend of ours," Quinn told her.

"Yes, he never brings women around, so we are geeked to see you," Erin told her.

Novah laughed as she looked their way. She exchanged numbers with Quinn and Erin and was soon leaving the studio with

252

Durand. After grabbing food from a local soul food spot, Durand went back with Novah to her home. They took a quick shower and retreated to Novah's bed. Durand answered calls from his lawyer as Novah picked over her macaroni and cheese.

The food smelled delicious, but the thought of eating food made her want to hurl again.

"My mom loved the spa party. I know she was in there wilding out with her girls," Durand said as he put his phone away.

Novah thought back on meeting Durand's young, vivacious mother and she laughed. His mom and her friends were a lively bunch.

"She was, and she looks so young."

Durand sat his food onto the marble nightstand and looked at Novah.

"She is. She had me when she was twelve. She gave me up for adoption, and I didn't meet her until six years ago," he revealed.

Novah stared at him with wide eyes not sure what to say.

"When I was younger, I hated her. I felt like an orphan until I met Trill and Malano. They was in the group home with me. We ran the streets together and eventually shacked up with Trill's bm. Her grandmother for some damn reason allowed for us to sleep in her basement. It had to be God, but even then, we was reckless. Jacking niggas and shit that's how I was shot. Falling saved my life though."

Novah caressed his hairy cheek.

"You're blessed, and that's why you're still here. How did you get over hating your mom?"

Durand shrugged.

"When she found me at one of my shows, I was so happy to see her that I let it go. We'd lost so many years together. I didn't have it in me to hate her anymore. I needed that love. That shit was like the missing puzzle piece. When we connected life changed for the better. Yeah, I had money and shit, but I wasn't happy. Meeting her and reconnecting with that side of my family gave me the kind of happiness that you can't pay for."

"Wow," Novah murmured having a new respect for Durand.

It took courage and strength to forgive, and she was happy to see that he was mature enough to do such a thing.

"My family life wasn't like yours per se. I grew up in a middle-class family, and my parents were the picture-perfect couple to me. They hated when I started doing videos, but they loved me enough to let me make my own mistakes. When I met Carter, my dad told me he wasn't the one," Novah said and dropped her gaze down to her ruffled duvet.

Durand kissed Novah's cheek, and she smiled at him. He seemed to know to do the right thing at the right time.

"He said that he didn't love me, and I ignored him. I guess what you said back at your place is kind of true. I fell in love with what I thought Carter could be. I wanted so badly to have what my parents had that I was willing to recreate that with any man. Even the wrong one."

Durand moved Novah's food into the nightstand and pulled her onto his lap. Her t-shirt rode up as he massaged her bare bottom.

"None of us are perfect. Everything happens for a reason. Without him, you wouldn't have your sons."

And without you, I wouldn't have this new baby.

Novah shook her head to clear her thoughts. Durand began to kiss her neck as her cellphone rung.

"Come with me to New York tomorrow. I'll have you back before your lil dudes come home," he said into her neck before tonguing it down.

Novah felt her mouth grow watery and she sighed.

"I'll have to see. I do have a business baby."

Baby?

The term of endearment made her frown but had the opposite effect on Durand. Novah eased off his lap. As she rushed to her bathroom her cellphone begin to ring. Novah ignored the call and turned the water on so that she could vomit in peace.

Once Novah was sure her stomach couldn't throw up anymore, she brushed her teeth. As she exited her bathroom, Durand sat at the foot of her bed with his phone pressed to his ear. His eyes lifted to her and she gave him a small smile.

"Ma, somebody blowing you up," he told her.

Novah grabbed her phone as her mom called her cell.

"Hey, ma. Everything okay?"

"No, Karter is in the hospital! He had an allergic reaction to some food that stupid ass Melanie cooked. We're at the Henry Ford in Bloomfield," her mom replied.

Novah ended the call and quickly tossed on her ripped jeans. Durand sat his phone down and stared at her.

"You good?"

Novah's chest heaved up and down as she took a second to look at Durand.

"No, my mom said that one of my sons had an allergic reaction to some food. I have to go check on him."

Durand jumped up and rushed to place on his clothes as well. Together they exited Novah's home and got into Durand's truck. Novah held Durand's hand tightly as he raced to the hospital.

"He's good. Relax," he assured her quietly.

Novah nodded with her left leg bouncing. Her babies had been blessed in the health department. They rarely caught colds and to know her son had eaten something involving seafood had her heated. It was the only thing he was allergic too, and she knew because she'd had him tested for it a year ago after he'd taken some shrimp off her plate.

Back then he'd only caught a fever, but the doctor let Novah and Carter know that it could potentially kill him if he injected too much.

Novah's teeth gritted as she thought of Carter and Melanie.

"First week in and they already have my baby at the fucking hospital. I'm fucking them up," she declared.

Durand glanced over at her and lightly squeezed her hand.

"Don't do anything that could help his case. Just keep the paper trail and remain calm. I found this lawyer from here that has a good winning streak. He's high as hell, but I think he can help you. I'm waiting on him to call my mom back now."

Novah turned to Durand and frowned.

"Your mom?" she asked with an angry bite to her question.

Durand chuckled as he looked over at her.

"Calm down man. I know you pissed but going in there on a hundred won't be good for you, and yeah, she's like my assistant you would say. I have her do little shit, and she likes it. You don't mind that I told her, do you?"

Novah thought of Durand's mother and shook her head. His mom seemed like she was a genuinely good person and had been nice to Novah the entire time she'd been at the spa party.

"No and sorry for the attitude. I'm not feeling well, and with this, on my mind, I feel like I'ma throw up again," she admitted.

Durand nodded as he pulled up to the hospital.

"Just relax sexy," he said glancing over at her.

After parking and entering the hospital it took Novah five minutes to locate her family. Her mom, sister, and Billie along with her cousin Arquez sat in the ER. On the other side of the room sat Carter and his people. Novah could feel Melanie burning a hole through her as she hugged her mom.

"I wanna go slap that bitch," Novah whispered to Normani.

Normani rubbed Novah's back lovingly.

"You and me both. Slap some common sense into her ugly ass. Just relax cause we gone pull up on her," Normani replied.

"Aye, chill out," Durand said rubbing Novah's arm.

Novah pulled back from her hug and went to Durand's side. Since Carter, she hadn't brought another man home. It felt weird in a sense because she had no clue what the hell, they were doing but she was also comfortable with him. More relaxed than she'd ever been with a man and that scared her as well.

"Everyone this is Durand my...my—"

"Close friend. It's nice to meet y'all," Durand said and dapped up Arquez who wore a small smirk on his handsome face.

Novah blushed as her mother gave her the side eye and before she could bask in the glow of introducing her family to Durand the nurse walked over.

"I was told the mother was here," the male nurse said with a blank look on his face.

Novah walked up to him and nodded.

"Where is my baby?"

"Right this way," he replied and walked away.

Novah glanced back at Durand, and he winked at her. She sighed as she walked off headed after the nurse. Carter met them halfway and stared Novah down as they headed for the room.

"Why the fuck you bring that hoe ass nigga up here? Huh!"

Novah and the male nurse stopped walking to look at Carter. Carter held a look of pure hatred on his face for Novah as he glared down at her.

261

"Make that muthafucka leave right now," he demanded lowly.

"Sir you will have to calm down," the nurse said looking Carters way.

Carter waved off the nurse and reached for Novah's arm. A large hand pressing against Novah's back made her jump. She glanced behind her and sighed when her eyes connected with Durand's.

The anger radiating off Carter could be felt a mile away as he glared Durand's way. Durand moved around Novah and held his hand out.

"We done bumped into each other a few times but never like this. I'm —"

"Did it look like I was interested in meeting you? Fuck outa my face," Carter vented and walked off.

Novah clutched Durand's hand tightly. She looked to the male nurse, and he stared down at her with an empathetic gaze.

"Your son is fine. He ingested shellfish, and it caused him to have an allergic reaction. I am warning you now that his face is slightly swollen, but he's okay. It's a good thing the babysitter called when she did," he told her.

Babysitter?

Shellfish?

Novah's mind was swirling with venomous thoughts. She swallowed hard and nodded. She grabbed onto Durand's arm for support, and the nurse led them into Karter's hospital room.

"Oh, my baby," Novah said as she rushed over to her peacefully sleeping, son.

"He's getting ready for discharge. The medicine made him drowsy," the nurse told her.

"I'd like a copy of the discharge papers," Novah said before going over to her son.

She kissed his handsome face as Durand rubbed her back. Just seeing her son in such a state made her sad. Broke her heart in a sense because she knew this would happen. It may have been small to some people, but Novah didn't want her boys to suffer in any sort of way. Carter wanted the kids more, and already he was fucking up.

The sad thing was she wasn't surprised.

"He's good," Durand said lowly.

His words relaxed Novah, and again she was grateful for his presence. She peered back at him and laughed lightly.

"I'm sure you're ready to run for the hills," she joked.

Durand shook his head while frowning.

"Your ex not shit for me to worry about. I wish I could have met your boys in a different way. Where your other son at?"

Novah's brows pinched together, and she sighed. She shrugged as she took a step back.

"Probably with Carter and his people. Let me go see."

As they exited the room, Carter stood against the opposite wall facing the hospital door. With his cellphone sitting in his hand he peered at Novah intently. All anger gone from his visage he cleared his throat.

"Let me holla at you real quick. Okay?"

Novah rolled her eyes. Carter was like Doctor Jekyll and Mr. Hide. One minute he was unruly and crass and the next he was timid and sweet. She was sure she would never understand him.

"Carter what do you want and where is King?"

Carter stared at Durand briefly. His eyes lingered down to where Durand touched Novah's waist, and Novah watched him struggle to keep his cool.

"He's with my mom at the house. Can I talk to you alone? You ain't married to this nigga so he really shouldn't fucking be here?"

"I'll be with your people beautiful," Durand whispered in Novah's ear before walking away.

Novah watched Durand walk off before looking at Carter. The second Durand was out of her line of sight. Carter was rushing upon her. He grabbed her hand aggressively and pulled her into

Karter's room. Novah struggled to break free from his hold as she stepped back away from him.

"Carter what the hell is wrong with you?" she snapped glaring at him.

Carter's chest heaved up and down as he glared back at her.

"You fucking that nigga? You gave him my pussy?"

Novah's head whipped back as amazement washed over her pretty face. She held her head as she stared up at him.

"Are you fucking serious? You have a whole wife, and you wanna know if I'm fucking him? It's none of your business who I'm fucking! How did you allow for our son to eat shellfish and since when did you get a babysitter?"

Carter placed his hands in his pockets and licked his lips. His face relaxed, and his smug attitude returned.

"Shit, I had a few extra dollars since my child support was cut, so Mel decided to hire somebody. We was out on a date, and the babysitter accidentally gave him that. I told Mel to make a list of food that they couldn't eat, but she forgot. You don't have to make a big deal out of this shit."

Novah shook her head. There was so many things she saw wrong with his words that she didn't know where to begin. She took a moment to compose herself before responding.

"Carter, I can't do this with you right now. I just can't but know that the judge will be hearing about this. I will get this order reversed."

Novah turned to walk out of the room, and Carter grabbed her arm roughly. He tightened his grip as he pulled her back to him.

"Novah I let a lot of the shit you do slide. You wanted us to break up, and eventually, I accepted that. You wanted to cut the pussy off, and again I let you do that, but this is where I draw the line ma. You gotta be out of your fucking mind if you think I'ma let you parade this nigga around my sons and me. We a family. Not you and that nigga. Let him go before shit gets ugly. I don't give a fuck who he is. I got niggas on speed dial that can make shit happen immediately. Cut that nigga off before it's too late baby. It'll be for the best, and if you do that, then I can maybe slide you a few more

267

dollars every week with your other money. You do something for me, and I'll do something for you," he whispered in her ear.

Novah snatched away from Carter and left out of the room. All the peace Durand had carried into her spirit was gone just like that. Carter was once again bringing drama to her that she didn't want or need.

8

#letmeexplain

The lights were dimmed low as everyone stood quietly inside of the large banquet hall. For the night, the room had been transformed into a real-life throwback scene. One of Dreux's favorite movies was Harlem Nights. Billie loved it as well, but she enjoyed the flick because of her baby.

Everyone's attire was reminiscent of the classic hit movie including Billie. She wore a vintage black gown that reached her ankle. Her hair had been done up in pin curls while red lipstick stained her lips. She smiled wide as she waited for the man of the hour to enter into the room.

"He's coming right now!" Deidra yelled looking stunning in the royal blue dress that she wore a feather headgear with.

Billie nodded. Seconds later Dreux stepped into the room with low lids. Beside him was his brother Donny. Both men looked handsome in their black Tom Ford tux's.

"Surprise!" everyone in the room yelled

Dreux jumped, and Donny patted his back.

"We got your ass boy! Happy Birthday, nigga!" Donny exclaimed and pulled Dreux into a hug.

Billie smiled with watery eyes as she watched the scene. Donny had been home for a week, and it was still surreal. She had sadly gotten used to him being behind bars but was glad to see him out of the cell.

She could only hope that his hustling days was behind him.

"Thank you, God," Deidra said beside Billie.

She walked off towards Dreux and Billie bid her time. She watched Dreux hug all his family even some of the member she knew he didn't like before his low, red-rimmed eyes found her. A sexy smirk covered his face as he headed her way.

"Don't forget what we discussed baby. I'm not ready for the family to know about you all," Deidra whispered to Billie before walking away.

Billie sighed at her words. Her court date had been pushed back another month, and Malachi's verbal abuse had reached an all-time low. She was over all the bullshit happening in her life, and she wanted to vent to her man about it. She also wanted to reveal to him that she'd helped Malachi pay him off. The secrets were killing her, and with Deidra adding more skeletons to her already full closet she could feel her anxiety with the situation mounting.

"Bring your sneaky, sexy ass here," Dreux said walking up on her.

Billie giggled until she replayed his words in her head.

"What do you mean sneaky?"

Dreux licked his lips as he gave her a deliberate once-over.

"Didn't you put this together and not tell me about it? That's sneaky as fuck, and I don't like that shit," he said and smiled at her.

Billie laughed. She shook off her nervousness and pushed his hand away.

"Babe not with your people in here."

Dreux's brows pulled together. He shook his head as he pulled Billie into his arms. Billie hugged him as she watched Malachi's mom stare over at them.

"I'm done with that hiding shit. You know, that right?"

Billie sighed.

"But court is coming up, and I don't need the drama. Please do this for me. A few more months then we can tell him," she pleaded.

Dreux's hands slid up and down Billie's back. He slapped her ass once before letting her go. She could tell from the look in his eyes that he wasn't happy.

"You know I never tripped about any of that shit. My people called me when I was away, ma. They told me that you was falling through to kick it with him, and I let it ride. I knew your heart, Billie. I knew that even if you was smiling in my cousins face it was cause you was mad at me..." Dreux stopped talking and cleared his throat. "Even after the baby shit happened, I brushed it off. That shit hurt deep. The only fucking kid you were supposed to be popping out was mine. Still, I let it slide. I made excuses for your ass. Even though you gave that nigga what was supposed to belong to me. I love the fuck out of you, but I'm starting to wonder just how much you love me? I'ma fuck with you later," he said and walked away.

Billie's eyes watered over, and a few tears fell down her face as Dreux walked away from her. They never spoke on her dealings with Malachi, but she knew that eventually, it would come out. She found a seat in the crowded hall and sat down.

For hours Billie watched Dreux chill with his family and pretend she wasn't there. She regretted letting Novah slide when she claimed to be too sick to come because she was bored as shit as she sat by herself at the round table.

"Happy Birthday nigga!" Malachi said loudly catching Billie's attention.

Billie looked up, and when her eyes landed on Dreux's old friend Kylie, she frowned. Kylie had once been a big problem for Billie and Dreux. Dreux had slept around with her while away at school and Malachi had informed Billie of that. Although she didn't have a relationship with Dreux, she'd still been hurt.

Billie's eyes landed on the small person beside Kylie, and her heart momentarily stopped beating. She watched Dreux looked from Kylie to the minor child, a girl with long curly hair and big bright eyes and Billie rose to her feet.

"What the fuck is going on?" Dreux asked as Billie walked up.

Malachi clad in a clean black tux with a fresh haircut and big smile glanced over at Billie. He chuckled as he looked back to Dreux.

"I ran into her online, and she asked me about you. Said that she needed to tell you some real important shit, so I flew her out," he replied.

Billie looked at Kylie, the pretty woman that held a strong resemblance to the actress Serayah Mcneill and they stared at one another.

"Hi," Kylie spoke quietly with a cocky look to her beautiful face.

Billie ignored the greeting and peered down at the child. She didn't see any semblance of the man she loved in the small girl, but she knew looks meant nothing. She'd seen enough of the Maury Povich show to know that looks didn't matter.

"Dreux lets leave," Billie said grabbing his arm.

Suddenly the room was beginning to spin as she stared at her man. What was supposed to be a good night had been everything but that. She was ready for it to be over and no matter what Dreux was coming home with her to their home.

Dreux sighed. He glanced down at the small girl once more, and his mother and aunt walked over along with his uncle.

"Nephew what kind of Jerry Springer shit you got going on in here," his uncle Larry cracked.

A few people chuckled, but Billie didn't find shit funny about it. She glared over at the man that had always been nothing but nice to her, and she frowned.

"It's not even like that Larry so calm down," she told him.

Malachi's mom frowned as she moved around her oldest brother.

"Now, Billie I love you, but you will watch how you speak to him," Cindy told her.

Billie waved Cindy off, and Malachi glared over at Billie.

"Look you can get the fuck out if you wanna trip. Nobody invited your lush, bitch ass anyway," he said loudly.

Dreux's disposition went from calm to irate in a matter of minutes. He moved Billie out of the way and before Malachi could make a run for it, he was on his ass. Dreux handled Malachi as if he weighed nothing as he pumped his fist into his face.

"What the fuck you call her nigga? Don't you ever in your fucking life disrespect her!" Dreux yelled brutally attacking Malachi.

"Oh my God! Stop him!" Deidra yelled.

Billie stood by quietly as she watched the scene unfold. She always knew Dreux could beat Malachi's ass but had never imagined it going that far.

"Aye! Aye, calm down!" Donny yelled pulling his brother off a savagely beaten up Malachi.

Cindy ran over to help her son stand up, and Malachi pushed her away. He licked his bloody lip as his left eye swelled up. His chest heaved up and down as he glared at Dreux.

"You gone fight me over my baby momma? What kind of nigga is you? She ain't shit but a drunk, and we all know that shit except you! I used this hoe for money and nothing else. How the fuck you think I was able to pay you back that money for the loan?" he asked and chuckled darkly.

Billie's eyes widened as Dreux glared over at her. She slowly shook her head, and Malachi laughed harder.

"Aye, this bitch ain't shit but a lying ass broad. I can't believe you still want her ass. She been fucking me anyway," he lied to Dreux.

Billie stepped towards Dreux, and he shook his head.

"Stay right there, ma. I'm not even bout to believe you was fucking him, but did you give him that money?" he asked while breathing hard himself.

Billie's shoulders sagged, and Malachi laughed.

"Told you nigga!" he quipped loudly.

Dreux glared over at him and tried to snatch from his brother's tight hold.

"I should kill your fat ass!" he snarled.

Deidra began to cry as she watched the scene unfold. Cindy glared over at her and shook her head.

"See what happened? You had them damn boys by my man, and they've done nothing but ruined our lives. If it wasn't for him, Billie would be with Malachi. You ain't shit Deidra!" she yelled.

Everyone in the room looked at Cindy as she began to cry. Dreux, Donny, and Malachi stood in shock as their uncle Larry shook his head.

"Cindy what the fuck is your drunk ass talking about now?" he asked.

Cindy wiped her face as Deidra looked at her sadly.

"No! You don't get to make me feel bad for what you've done. I want this whole family to know right now that my only sister fucked my man for years and she had to bastard ass boys by him. Our boys that should be cousins are fucking brothers!" Cindy yelled and stormed out of the room.

Malachi took a step back not believing it as Deidra looked to her sons. Donny stormed out of the room as Dreux glared at his mother.

"Is it true ma?" he asked lowly.

The music had long ago been cut off.

Deidra nodded with tears cascading down her face. She opened her mouth to speak, and Dreux walked off. Billie ran after him and caught him as he walked down the hall.

"Dreux wait! Baby please!" she begged.

She was in shock and didn't know what to say but what she did know was that her man needed her, and she needed him.

"Dreux please," she begged pulling on his arm.

Dreux stared straight ahead while breathing hard.

"Bethany let my arm go. I'll hit you in a few days," he said, and after pulling away from her grip, he was gone.

Billie's legs shook as she watched her man exit the banquet hall. Her cellphone vibrated in her purse, and she quickly retrieved it. Hopes of it being Dreux died when she watched Normani's name slide across the screen.

"Hello," she answered sadly.

Normani breathed into the phone before whimpering.

"Billie, I need your help. I think I killed Tru," she

whispered, and the last bit of strength Billie had fled from her body.

She dropped down to the ground and cried as hard as she

could.

to be continued....

Book Discussion Questions

1. Do you think Dreux is going to breakup with Billie?

2. Were you shocked to learn Dreux and Malachi was brothers?

3. How do you think Carter will act once he learns of Novah's pregnancy?

4. Do you think Durand got Novah pregnant on purpose?

5. Why do you think Normani attempted to kill Tru?